FLINT BOOK 5:
BACK IN THE HOOD

FLINT BOOK 5: BACK IN THE HOOD

TREASURE HERNANDEZ

www.urbanbooks.net

Urban Books, LLC
78 East Industry Court
Deer Park, NY 11729

Flint Book 5: Back in the Hood Copyright © 2009 Urban
Books, LLC

ISBN 13: 978-1-60162-454-3
ISBN 10: 1-60162-454-9

First Mass Market Printing June 2011
First Trade Paperback Printing June 2009
Printed in the United States of America

10 9 8 7 6 5 4 3 2 1

*This is a work of fiction. Any references or similarities to ac-
tual events, real people, living, or dead, or to real locales are
intended to give the novel a sense of reality. Any similarity in
other names, characters, places, and incidents is entirely coin-
cidental.*

Distributed by Kensington Publishing Corp.
Submit Wholesale Orders to:
Kensington Publishing Corp.
C/O Penguin Group (USA) Inc.
Attention: Order Processing
405 Murray Hill Parkway
East Rutherford, NJ 07073-2316
Phone: 1-800-526-0275
Fax: 1-800-227-9604

Acknowledgments

First and foremost, I would like to thank God for all the blessings he has bestowed upon me.

I would like to thank all my fans for all the letters and pictures. It has kept me going.

Please send all letters to Urban Books, they will make sure I get them.

Holla at your girl!!!!

Treasure Hernandez
c/o Urban Books, LLC
1199 Straightpath
West Babylon, NY 11704

Love & Peace,
Treasure

FLINT BOOK 5:
BACK IN THE HOOD

Chapter One

Malek paced back and forth in his extravagant living room, while Mitch stood at the door watching his partner go crazy.

"Where the fuck is she, fam?" Malek asked, his voice a mixture of concern and anger as he dialed Halleigh's cell phone number for the millionth time. "Why she got a phone, if she ain't gon' ever answer the mu'fucka?"

Malek snapped his phone closed and grabbed his Sean John coat. His thoughts went from one extreme to the other as he tried to reason with himself about Halleigh's absence. Malek loved Halleigh with all that he was, and she had never given him a reason to distrust her or shown him any shade in the past, but just the simple fact that she used to trick with niggas had him going crazy. Under normal circumstances, he knew she would never step out on him, but because of her history as a Manolo Mami, he was worried.

Treasure Hernandez

That old cliché about a man not being able to turn a ho into a housewife, for some reason, was now haunting him.

He didn't want her reverting back to her old ways, and made it a point to do everything he thought possible to keep her on the up-and-up, seeing to it that she lacked nothing, especially when it came to sex.

He closed his eyes and could picture Halleigh being pleased by another man. He could hear the moans escaping her lips, the same moans that blessed his ears every time he stroked her right. "I'ma murder a mu'fucka tonight, fam." Malek grabbed his car keys and stormed out of the house.

"Where you going, bro? Your chick ain't fucking around on you. Calm down and just think about it. We talking about Halleigh here, not some chickenhead off the street," Mitch reminded him. "She probably just lost track of time, kicking it with some of her girlfriends," Mitch added, trying to reason with Malek.

"Girlfriends," Malek whispered to himself. He knew Halleigh didn't rock with a lot of chicks. The only friend she ever mentioned was Tasha. That didn't soothe any of Malek's concerns, seeing as Tasha was an ex-Manolo Mami as well.

I hope she ain't sliding back into her old ways, messing around with Tasha, he thought. Out loud, he said, "Roll with me for a minute. I think I know where she might be."

Malek left the house, and with Mitch in the passenger's seat, he rolled to Tasha's apartment complex just outside of the city. He had only been there once, when he had dropped Halleigh off to pick up some of her things, and he was hoping Tasha still stayed there.

He sped through the illuminated city streets, his brand-new 6 Series decorating the hood as he passed by. Malek hit a button on his panel, and a compartment slid out of his console, exposing various-sized money rolls, a blunt, and a pistol. He grabbed one of the money rolls and tossed it to Mitch.

Mitch caught the roll then looked up at his boy with confusion on his face. He had no idea what the money was for.

"For that work you put in on the Genesis center," Malek explained, referring to the shooting that had taken place at the local rehab center. The place was cutting into Malek's business, and after the director refused to shut it down, Malek had decided to make her understand that she had no choice. "Good looking out on that. I saw it on the eleven o'clock news. We shouldn't have no more problems from Moses or her cause. Niggas trying to fly straight hurts my pockets, nah mean?"

Mitch didn't respond. He merely nodded and counted out the five stacks Malek had just hit him with.

Moments later, Malek pulled into Tasha's apart-

ment community. "I'll be right back, fam." He got out of the car and headed toward what he hoped was Tasha's place.

He approached the front door and almost knocked it off the hinges with his hard, police-like knock, more out of anxiety than anger. He couldn't fathom the thought of Halleigh back-sliding and making a fool out of him.

People already thought he was off his game by making a Manolo Mami his wifey. The old saying "you can't turn a ho into a housewife" resonated tough in the hood, so he knew his relationship with Halleigh was a topic for discussion around the way. Because of his soft spot for Halleigh, some fools had misinterpreted that to mean he was a soft nigga altogether, testing him on a daily. On more occasion than one, he had to prove himself to be anything but. Sometimes he didn't know who he was trying to prove it to, though: the streets or himself. Nonetheless, he wasn't about to let everything he'd risked for Halleigh be in vain.

He had disregarded her lifestyle once because he knew what had forced her into the streets. It wasn't like she had planned on working for Manolo. A bad set of circumstances had put her out there, and once she was reunited with Malek, she left that life behind—or so he thought until now, when he couldn't get a hold of her. If he found out she was disloyal now, there would be no excuse. He provided her with everything and

made good on his promise to take care of her. She was living lavishly and was in a spot where many females wanted to be.

If she's on the other side of this door, I'm cutting her the fuck off, Malek thought as he banged on the door.

Tasha snatched open the door wearing sweatpants, a sports bra, and her hair wrapped. It was obvious that Malek had awakened her. "What the fuck?" she spat, her mug all twisted up.

She looked over Malek's shoulder, as if looking to see if anyone else was with him. She couldn't imagine why he would be on her doorstep. She knew this nigga had balls, but not this big to show up where she laid her head, knowing the loss he'd caused her.

"Why are you banging my shit down like you the police or something?" She folded her arms and stood waiting for an answer. She hated him for what he had done to her brother. What Tasha didn't know was that Malek had killed her brother in self defense. Maury and a chick named Mimi had set him up, but he got the best of them in the end. Still, none of that would have mattered to Tasha. All she cared about was that her brother was dead, and the man responsible was standing in front of her now. If looks could kill, Malek would've dropped where he stood.

"I'm looking for Halleigh. She ain't been home all night. It's four in the morning. I know

she been out tricking with you." Malek pushed past Tasha as if he were walking into his own house.

"Nigga, I don't know you like that. Don't come at me out the side of your neck. Your bitch ain't here. I don't rock with Halleigh as long as she's fucking with you." Tasha went to retrieve her phone.

Malek was paying absolutely no attention to the words coming out of Tasha's mouth as he walked all over the apartment looking for his girl. "Halleigh?" he called out, opening door after door.

"You need to get out! No, wait. As a matter of fact,"—A sinister smile spread across her lips—"you can stay. I got something for your ass." She picked up her phone and began to dial Sweets' number.

Sweets was in charge of the South Side until he had Jamaica Joe, his North Side rival, killed. He went underground for a while after the hit, and that's when Malek stepped in and took over his blocks. Now Malek was on top of both the North and South sides, and Sweets wasn't having it. He teamed up with Halleigh's ex-pimp, and they were working on a plan to take Malek out. Sweets and Manolo had been trying to touch Malek for a minute, and what better opportunity than for Tasha to serve him up on a silver platter. Malek had come right to her.

Just as she was about to click on her cordless,

the phone rang in her hand. Only one person called her on her home phone, and that was Manolo. She answered the phone with a smirk on her face, not even looking at the caller ID. "Manolo, I—"

The voice on the other end of the phone line interrupted Tasha. "Hello, I'm calling for Tasha Smith regarding your sister, Halleigh."

"Halleigh?" Tasha's eyes then quizzically darted toward Malek.

Malek stopped in his tracks at the mention of Halleigh's name. He slowly walked toward Tasha as she turned her attention back to the caller on the other end of the phone.

"Uh, hello," Tasha greeted with a stammer.

"Yes, is this Tasha Smith?"

Taken aback, Tasha responded, "Uh yeah . . . yeah, this is Tasha."

"You are listed as Halleigh's emergency contact in our hospital records. Halleigh was shot today, and—"

"Shot? What? Hold on." Tasha put the phone on hold and looked at Malek.

She hated Malek and everything he stood for, but she felt an obligation to tell him the news she'd just received. She wasn't surprised that the hospital had reached out to her instead of Malek because, back in the day, Manolo had ensured that Tasha was the contact person for all of his working girls, just in case a john ever decided to get rough. Tasha wanted to be an ass-

hole and leave Malek wondering where his girl was, but if Halleigh was dying, she didn't think she deserved to die alone.

She sighed from frustration at her hatred for Malek, but her conflicting loyalty to her old friend prevailed. Tasha took the phone off hold and continued her conversation with the caller, learning a few more details, including exactly what hospital Halleigh was at. Afterward, Tasha hung up the phone and turned toward Malek.

"Why you storming up in here accusing Halleigh of fucking around?" Tasha said heatedly. "She's laid up in the county hospital. She's been shot, Malek. Now see yourself out." She pointed at her front door.

The words hit Malek like a thousand darts to the heart, and he backpedaled out of Tasha's apartment without saying another word. He didn't know what to think. He closed his eyes and washed his hands down his face and shook his head. He hoped that once he opened his eyes, he'd be lying in bed next to Halleigh, waking up from what had to be a nightmare, but when he opened them, there he stood, right there in front of Tasha's apartment.

"Damn," was the only word that escaped Malek's mouth as he stood frozen in his own thoughts. *Is she a'ight? How did this happen?* He realized he was wasting time standing there, so he snapped out of it and ran and jumped into his car. He sped out of the parking lot like a bat out of hell.

"Whoa! Fam, slow this mu'fucka down," Mitch stated as he looked at Malek.

Malek, his mind fixed on thoughts of Halleigh, had forgotten all about Mitch even being out there in the car. "She's been shot, fam. She's pregnant and could be dying, and I thought she was out doing dirt," Malek whispered regretfully. He banged his fist against the steering wheel.

It was then that Malek knew he would have to fully forgive Halleigh and renew his trust in her. This "hard" role he had been trying to play wasn't becoming of him, nor was it by any means fair to Halleigh. He had no idea where the college-bound Malek who used to be the star of the high school basketball team had gone. He had to be somewhere underneath that hard-ass exterior Malek donned himself in on a daily. Halleigh, to this day, was still the same Halleigh he had fallen in young love with. So, if he was going to spend the rest of his life with her, then he had to be real about it. Living in the past wasn't going to get them anywhere.

Constantly thinking of what Halleigh used to do and who she used to do it with had clouded Malek's judgment and was making him go crazy. Halleigh needed him, and he was out wildin' over something she hadn't even done. Once again, he hit the steering wheel forcefully, his anger shifting to a new place.

"Whoever did this is dead. On my mother, I'm going to catch a couple bodies when I find out who hurt her."

"I'll put the word out," Mitch said as he shook his head in disgust.

Mitch secretly envied Malek because of his relationship with Halleigh. He'd heard the stories of the young couple's history and knew he could never break their bond, but he had been interested in Halleigh since the first time he'd seen her. The fact that he'd twisted her out in the back of his car when she was working for Manolo was his own private joke that he often chuckled at. Malek would be bragging about his lady, and silently Mitch would be thinking, *I know, nigga. I've had her.* But having her once wasn't enough for Mitch. He wanted her permanently.

He had tried his hand at Halleigh after she got back with Malek, but she was loyal to her man. She'd turned down every advance Mitch made toward her; still, the fact that she never told Malek always gave Mitch hope. He was just waiting for Malek to mess up. Then he would get him out of the picture for good and take the streets away from him, along with his woman.

Chapter Two

The drive to the hospital seemed to take forever, but fifteen minutes later Malek was pulling into the emergency room parking lot of the county hospital. He double-parked right in front of the entrance and hopped out, leaving Mitch in the passenger's seat.

"I'ma park your whip. I'll be up in a minute!" Mitch yelled as he watched Malek disappear into the building.

Malek approached the reception area and bypassed the line of people waiting in front of him, worry and concern plastered on his face. People mumbled and complained about Malek's ditching the line, but he tuned them out. All he wanted to hear was that his baby was all right— both of them. He said to the young white intake nurse who sat behind the desk, "My girlfriend was brought here for a gunshot wound. Her name's Halleigh. What room is she in?"

She rolled her eyes and then looked down at some paperwork in front of her. "I'm sorry, sir, but you have to wait in line like everyone else. There are sick people and concerned relatives waiting for information just like you." She looked past him at the line and yelled, "Next!"

"Look, lady, I'm next! I don't care about a line. I need to know what room my girl is in. She could be dying while I'm down here arguing with you!" he shouted, more out of emotion than anger. He had to keep it together.

A doctor passing by heard the commotion and stopped. "Is there a problem?"

"Hey, my man," Malek started, "please, I'm just trying to get to my girlfriend. She was shot today and—"

The doctor cut him off. "Are you here for Halleigh . . ." The doctor flipped through the charts in his hands to find Halleigh's last name.

"Yeah, that's her name," Malek said before the doctor could finish his sentence.

The doctor looked down at the intake nurse. "It's okay. I'll take him to her." He began to walk, and Malek closely followed his lead. "We've been trying to reach someone for her since she was admitted yesterday evening."

"What happened to her? Is she a'ight?"

"She's okay. She's a very strong young woman. We had a lot of gunshot victims come in yesterday as a result of the Genesis shooting. She was one of the lucky ones. Why anyone would want to shoot up a rehab facility is beyond me."

Malek's heart hit his stomach, and he stopped walking. He had put in the order for the Genesis shooting, and Halleigh had gotten touched behind it.

She wasn't supposed to be there, he thought.

"Is everything all right?" the doctor asked.

Malek's eyes had watered over from guilt, but he continued following the doctor. "Yeah, everything's good, doc," he lied. "Can I see her?"

The doctor stopped at a closed door and said, "She's right inside. She's in some pain, but she'll be fine."

"And the baby?"

"The baby is fine," the doctor answered with a smile. "We were able to hear a very strong heartbeat."

Malek exhaled and rushed into the room, where Halleigh was lying, weak, tubes running into her arms. It killed him to know that she was in that state because of him.

He walked over to her bed slowly. Her face was so peaceful, so still, that if it weren't for the up-and-down movement of her chest, he would have sworn she had already left him behind. He placed his hand on her stomach and leaned his head onto her bedside. "I'm so sorry, Hal. I didn't know you were there. I didn't know you were at the rehab center. I swear to God, I'ma make this up to you. I'ma make it right."

He kicked himself for being so stupid. Before making a move, he should have made sure that she was tucked away safely, but he had no idea

she would be at the center. There was no reason for her to be . . . unless she was using again.

He dismissed that idea almost as quickly as it formed in his mind. He knew the symptoms of an addict, and Halleigh had none. No, she wasn't using, yet she had gotten aired out in the middle of the Genesis shootout. It didn't make sense to him, but he was just grateful that his lady was still breathing.

He felt Halleigh's hand wrap around his, and he looked at her in surprise.

"Hey," she said quietly, her voice scratchy and weak.

"Thank you," Malek whispered, lifting his eyes to the ceiling, acknowledging God's work. He had never been a Bible-toter, but he was so grateful for Halleigh's safety, he knew a greater power had to be at work. It wasn't the first time that some type of higher power had stepped in and saved the couple from the angel of death. As far as Malek was concerned, there wasn't anyone else he could give credit to but God. It certainly wasn't just plain old good luck. He knew better than anyone that luck had never been on their side. Ever since fate separated them and forced them to survive on the streets, both of them had faced death more than a few times. They had definitely experienced more than their share of bad luck.

* * *

Halleigh felt so tired. The medication they had her on was weighing her down, making her feel as if she had gained a thousand pounds overnight. It was even hard for her to move her mouth to talk, but she felt like she owed her man an explanation.

"Malek, I'm so sorry for lying to you. I wanted to tell you I had been going to Genesis, but I knew you would try to stop me."

"Why, Halleigh? Why would you be going there?" He tried not to be angry that she had been going to the place that was killing his street trade. This was not the time to be thinking about business.

"I have a friend there . . . Scratch. I was trying to help him kick his habit," she explained. "I wanted to let him know that someone cared. I thought it would help him get better. You know, the same way I knew someone cared about me." She forced her lips to curve into a slight smile, her sign of appreciation for Malek always being there for her. "That's what got me through. But I had no idea something like this would happen."

"Hal, when you didn't come home last night, I went crazy. Hearing that you were hurt was like a bullet to the chest, ma. I'm in love with you, and I'm so sorry I put you through this."

"You have nothing to be sorry for, baby." Halleigh gripped his hand tighter.

"Yes, I do." Malek swallowed hard, debating

whether he should tell Halleigh the real deal. But being the main one who insisted there be no secrets between them, he knew he had to fess up. So, he told her the miserable truth and hoped she could forgive him.

"Hal, I'm the one who gave the order to shoot up Genesis. I pushed the button."

"What?" she asked in confusion as she withdrew her hand from his.

Malek reached for it again. "Don't do that to me, Hal. I'm sorry. I had no idea you'd be there," he said.

"Why would you do something like that, Malek? How could you?"

"I didn't know you were there. I was stupid."

"And if I hadn't been there, the other people there didn't matter? There were kids in there, Malek! People who weren't bothering nobody. They were trying to get their lives together," she whispered harshly, tears filling her eyes.

It hurt her so bad to think that person she laid up with every night was responsible for the tragedy that had almost taken her life. Halleigh loved Malek to death, God knows she did, but he just seemed to be so hard and ruthless these days, nothing like the Malek who'd stolen her heart back in high school.

"I know, Hal. I know. Let's just focus on you getting better," Malek said, attempting to calm her down.

"No, Malek." Halleigh pulled away from his

touch. "You don't understand. My mother was in there," she cried.

Malek was shocked to hear Halleigh mention her mother, especially in a caring way. She was the reason Halleigh ended up on the streets in the first place. If it hadn't been for Sharina and her drug habit, everything might have turned out different. But obviously, Halleigh didn't hold a grudge.

"Yeah, I've hated her for a long time," Halleigh said, "but she was there, and I don't wish death on her. And my friend was in there."

"Hal—"Malek started, but she shot him a look that cut through him like a knife.

"I don't even know you right now," she said as a tear freed itself from her eyes.

Malek knew he couldn't really say anything that would make this better. Everything Halleigh had said was well deserved. He was nothing like the man he'd once dreamed of becoming.

The game was sucking him dry. Sometimes he didn't even recognize himself. He had come so far away from boyhood, but sometimes he still felt like he didn't know shit about being a real man. Back when he was headed for the NBA, he never imagined he could one day become a straight-up killer. But now, forced to survive on the streets, that's exactly what he was—and it had almost cost him everything.

"I know how you must feel, but please forgive me, Hal," he pleaded.

Halleigh shook her head as another tear fell. "I'm tired of this, Malek. I love you, but I don't know if I want my life to be like this. For so long I was living wrong, and you judged me for it. But who are you to judge anybody?" She closed her eyes and turned her head away from him.

Malek started to protest, but Halleigh didn't give him a chance to speak as she turned back to face him and then continued, "You don't have to lie and deny it. I can tell you still think about my past. You look at me, and a part of you can't get over the fact that I was a Manolo Mami. I've been working hard to regain your trust, Malek, but you can't throw stones when you live in a glasshouse. You ain't living right either. You shot up a building full of innocent people, Malek! How fucked-up is that?" Halleigh shook her head and waited for Malek to say something, but he didn't.

"Malek, I love you, and I know this isn't you. This isn't the real Malek." She looked him up and down. "This person standing in front of me, this person I've been living with isn't the Malek I know. I mean, you act like you've got something to prove to somebody, when all that's supposed to matter is me and you."

Finally finding his words, Malek spoke. "You gotta believe me, Hal. You and me is all that matters."

Halleigh, through the pain, tried her best to sit up as much as she could. "Do you really mean

that, Malek? I mean, if it really is just about me and you, then we have to leave this life alone."

A smile covered Halleigh's face, as if reminiscing. "Remember before, in high school, what our only goal was?"

Malek smiled and nodded.

"Me too. It was to get the hell out of Flint. So when did that all change? Why did it change?"

Malek shrugged.

"Then let's do it. Let's get out of this city before it swallows us whole. We can go somewhere and be us again. We can go back and be how we used to be before our lives spun out of control."

"Give it all up," Malek said more to himself than to Halleigh.

"Give it all up for me. You have enough money to be set for a while. Let's start over," Halleigh pleaded, getting worked up.

Malek stood over her and rubbed her head gently. "Is that what I have to do to keep you?"

A tear slid down Halleigh's face, and she shook her head. "This is what you have to do to save me, to save us. I can't live like this anymore."

Malek thought about her words for a minute. He couldn't say he really wanted to give up the streets—especially now, when he was just coming into his own. He was the king of the city, and he couldn't deny that he was becoming addicted to the power.

He let himself think about how big he could

become if he stayed in Flint. He could give Halleigh and the baby everything they'd ever dreamed of, and everyone would know his name. But then he looked down at his woman, who'd almost died because of him. No amount of money or power would have been able to bring her back.

It was time to give away the keys to the city. If he wanted to keep his woman safe, he'd have to give it all up and move on, whether he wanted to or not.

"Okay, Hal, I hear you. I'll get my affairs in order, and then we'll get ghost and kiss this city good-bye."

"Are you just saying that, or are you serious? Because do you know how many dudes from the street say they're gonna go legit but then turn around and let the streets keep pulling them back in?"

Both Halleigh and Malek let out a little chuckle. Then Malek said, "Girl, you been watching too much of *The Godfather*. Anyway, I'm serious. I mean it. I wouldn't lie to you, ma, about something like this." Malek bent down and kissed Halleigh on the forehead. "You gotta trust me on this."

Halleigh looked deeply into Malek's eyes. "Baby, I do trust you."

Malek smiled and kissed her again. "Get some sleep, and don't worry about anything. I'll take care of it."

Halleigh closed her eyes and shortly thereafter fell off to sleep, and Malek sat with her until the

nurses forced him to leave. When he finally emerged from Halleigh's room, he saw Mitch sprawled out in the waiting room, his coat thrown over his face.

Malek looked at the clock on the wall. It was nine o'clock in the morning. He had completely forgotten that Mitch was even with him, but he had a new respect for his right-hand man. Mitch had waited patiently throughout the night without complaint.

He approached Mitch and kicked his foot gently. "Yo, man, we outta here." Malek rubbed his red eyes. He had a lot on his mind and needed to get some sleep so he could wake up refreshed and analyze his situation.

He wasn't going to say anything to Mitch about his plan to leave Flint until he had all his ducks in order. Since Mitch knew all of Malek's business affairs anyway, he'd be the one to inherit the throne.

"How's Hal?" Mitch asked as he stood up and stretched. "She a'ight?"

"She was in the fucking rehab center. I had the mu'fucka shot up with her inside. Now she's laid up on the fifth floor," was all Malek could say, his voice cracking from emotion. Admitting to himself that Halleigh's circumstance was his fault was like taking a bullet himself.

"What?" Mitch asked. "What was she doing there? You should've made sure she was in pocket before you put that order in, fam. You know that. She should've been right under-

neath you, just so you were sure she wasn't in harm's way." Mitch's tone was more that of a concerned boyfriend than a supportive best friend.

Malek didn't like the way Mitch was coming at him, but he couldn't really get mad, because everything Mitch was saying was right. He didn't appreciate another nigga speaking on his relationship with Halleigh, but he was too tired to start anything. He held his tongue, unaware that Mitch had larceny in his heart.

"I know, fam, I know. Don't rub salt in it, my nigga." Malek extended his hand to Mitch.

Mitch embraced Malek and grabbed his coat as they began to leave. "I got to piss." Mitch tossed Malek his car keys. "Go grab the whip. I'll be out in a minute."

Malek nodded his head and exited the hospital.

Mitch headed over to the elevator. He looked around inconspicuously before pressing the call button, and then slipped into the space unnoticed as he headed to the fifth floor. He walked casually down the hall, peeking his head into each room until he saw Halleigh's silhouette in a darkened room. He knocked lightly but didn't wait to be invited in before he stepped into the room.

Both his slight knock and presence caused Halleigh to open her eyes from her light sleep.

"What's good, ma? How you feeling?" he

asked as he walked over to her and sat on the edge of her bed.

Halleigh sat up and nervously fidgeted with her hair. She never felt completely comfortable around Mitch because of the history they shared. She looked behind Mitch, expecting to see Malek walk through the door behind him. When he didn't, she asked, "What are you doing here?"

"I came here with Malek to check on you. I just want to make sure you're straight." Mitch looked over his shoulder to make sure the coast was clear. He turned his attention back to Halleigh and began to speak in a whisper. "Malek went a little bit crazy, Hal. I don't know what's up with him lately, so be careful, ma. I know you're with him now, but I care about you, and I don't want to see you caught out there on some bullshit."

Halleigh's eyebrows furrowed, and a look of confusion washed over her face. "What are you talking about, Mitch?"

Mitch began his infiltration into his comrade's relationship with the girl he truly had desires for. "Malek thought you were stepping out on him, Hal. He had you followed and then gave the order to have the building you were in shot up."

Halleigh didn't speak. She just lay there shaking her head.

"It's true, Halleigh," Mitch said convincingly.

"He knew you were inside. His jealousy over you is crazy. I don't want to see you hurt."

Mitch was manipulative. He knew he was planting seeds to cause problems in their relationship. His lies might not do much now, but they would remain in Halleigh's head until they manifested into a bigger problem. He was going to chip away at Halleigh's trust for Malek until he could snatch her, and then take the streets away from Malek.

"No, he wouldn't do that," Halleigh finally responded.

Mitch stood up and nodded as if he understood her choosing to be in denial over her boyfriend's true intentions on her life. He kissed the top of her head, even though she moved away from his touch. "I hear you, Halleigh. You're loyal. I know that's your man, but I just wanted to pull your coattail and tell you to be careful. I don't want to see you hurt. My offer still stands too. Whenever you're ready to leave your situation, you have somewhere to go," he stated before leaving her to her thoughts.

Halleigh thought about what Mitch had just told her, but she refused to believe him. *Malek would never do me like that on purpose.* She dismissed the idea and let the drugs the doctors had given her take her into a mind-numbing sleep.

Chapter Three

Malek hit the streets with full force. He knew that eventually he would have to let them go. Being a hustler was a full-time job, and although Halleigh was his wifey, the streets of Flint were his side bitch, his retreat, and he needed them almost as much as he needed Halleigh. He knew he couldn't just cut things off cold turkey, or else withdrawal would be a son of a bitch.

His connection to getting money was something Halleigh would never be able to understand. It was the only thing he had to hold on to that would keep him sane. Malek had blown an NBA contract by being stupid, and at one point, Halleigh wasn't around to lessen that pain and disappointment. His focus became his hustle, which led to his reign as second in command underneath Jamaica Joe. It filled up the spot in his heart where Halleigh was meant to be.

Now that she was back, she was asking him to

choose. The hood life or Hal? Which one was it going to be? Malek's guilt over the role he played in her injuries made him lean toward her. He just wanted to be with her.

For as long as he could remember, Halleigh had been the girl of his dreams. He remembered seeing her for the first time. In high school, she was a good girl. She wasn't too flashy, but always stayed fly in the latest teen fashions by Rocawear and Baby Phat. She was pretty without being over the top, and she wasn't into makeup and revealing clothing. She didn't need all the extras; she was who she was, which was perfect in Malek's eyes. They had formed a friendship first before they started kicking it, which explains why their bond was so strong.

When Malek first approached her, she wasn't feeling him. She later told him that she never thought a superstar like him would be interested in a girl like her; but it was her meek and humble qualities that drew him in like a magnet. Malek was used to groupies and hood rats approaching him daily. They all thought he was the one that would fly them out of the hood on a private jet with all of his potential NBA money. They saw him as a meal ticket, and were willing to do whatever it took to be the one he chose. Their efforts were useless because, although he accepted the ass and tricks of his groupies, he had no intention of making any of them his girl. He had never been "captain save-a-ho."

Malek knew that Halleigh would be his wife

before she'd ever agreed to go out with him. He felt that deeply for her, and the fact that she was a virgin was extra special to him. She was saving herself for him, but made it clear that he had to earn it. Halleigh never saw dollar signs when she looked at Malek; she saw love, and that's why he cherished her so much.

Fate just dealt them a different hand and separated them for a while.

A lot of things had changed since his puppy-love days with her. He wasn't the same. She definitely was not the same, yet here they were in the present, trying to make it work. Malek wondered if they could get back all they had lost, because neither of them was innocent anymore. Still, he knew he had to give it a chance. He loved her, and if he had to let the streets go in order to make her happy, he would regretfully do so.

He reached over to his passenger's seat and moved the cocaine-filled duffel bag to the backseat. He'd come to the decision that he'd give up the streets for her, to make sure the two of them would be straight when they started their new life together elsewhere. First, though, he had to get a few ki's off. Even if he was on his way out the game, he wasn't taking any losses.

The doctors said that Halleigh's hospital stay would be around three weeks, which gave him three weeks to get papered up.

Hand-over-fist sales were a thing of the past for Malek. He was a duffel-bag boy, but he was

anything but little. In the backseat of his car, he carried a life sentence with him—fifty kilos of cocaine. Jamaica Joe had already left him with a meal ticket, so he didn't have to work another day of his life if he didn't want to, but Malek wanted stupid money.

Malek wasn't trying to ball out for himself. He was trying to build generational wealth that he could pass down to his children and his children's children. He wanted security and was willing to put his life on the line to ensure that his family would be able to eat without struggling. He had watched his own mother fret over money for years. She was always robbing Peter to pay Paul, and that was something he refused to make Halleigh do. Now that she was pregnant with his baby, he felt obligated to take care of her forever.

Malek didn't have time to distribute the bricks on the streets. He couldn't hit anyone with consignment. He only had three weeks to get the dope off, and if he gave a nigga anything on credit and didn't get the return on his money, he would have to kill him, and that wasn't no front. That was on the real. He couldn't risk it. He couldn't jeopardize himself like that, because he had a girl and a baby on the way, and they were depending on him. Halleigh had given him an ultimatum, and he knew she meant what she'd said. In so many words, if Malek didn't retire from the dope game, then Halleigh would leave

him and take his seed with her. He couldn't have that.

He spun through the city streets, acknowledging his street fame, giving head nods to the corner hustlers who noticed him and showed love. He would miss the game, but not the treachery that came along with it. He had seen a lot of people murdered, trying to be boss, and he himself had taken a lot of lives on his way to the top. Now it was time to pass the crown, which he knew Mitch would be more than willing to accept—that is, after he helped Malek get off those fifty ki's.

"What's on your mind, Mitch? I've been trying to throw this pussy at you all morning, and you been brushing me off, acting all brand-new. What's up wit' you anyway?" Keesha fussed as she sat up on the bed in frustration and hit a strawberry blunt.

"Halleigh was in the rehab center when it got sh—"

Keesha didn't even let Mitch finish his sentence. She smacked her lips in disgust. "Halleigh? Why are you so concerned about Halleigh? I'm tired of every nigga in the city acting like that bitch pussy can't get funky. Let me remind you of something, baby boy: Halleigh is Malek's girl, and you work for Malek. You're like his little bitch almost," she said with a patronizing smirk.

"That mu'fucka say jump, and you and the rest of these small-time-ass niggas asking how high." Keesha choked on her words because of the weed smoke. As she held her head back to let the smoke ease slowly from her lips, she closed her eyes.

SLAP!

Mitch slapped the shit out of her, causing her to fall off the bed, the blunt falling on top of her and burning the side of her face.

"Let me tell you something, ma." Mitch got on top of her and gripped his hand around her throat. "I don't know how you talk to Manolo or that faggot-ass nigga, Sweets, but you better bite your tongue when you with me. You hear me?" Mitch said, spit flying in Keesha's face with every syllable. All Keesha could do was nod as the fear of death filled her eyes. Mitch released her with a jerk and got off her.

Keesha humbled up real quick, picking herself up from the floor timidly and holding her burning cheek. "I didn't mean nothing by it, boo," she said. "I'm just frustrated because I hate to see somebody in a spot they don't deserve. You know Malek wouldn't be where he is if it wasn't for Jamaica Joe. After Joe died, it was supposed to be you. You're not a right-hand man, baby. You're a star."

She walked over to Mitch and rubbed his back as she continued to blow his head up. "You've got to take your hood back. Sweets don't care if you run the North side, because you're about

your business. It's something in it for everybody; but Malek is still on that North versus South bullshit, and Sweets needs that nigga done.

"After you take out Malek, you'll be boss. Everybody in the city will be on your coattail, and just to show his gratitude, Sweets will cop all of the dope he sells to the South Side from you. It's a win-win situation. All you have to do is get Malek out of the picture." Keesha went and picked up the smoldering blunt from the floor, took a puff, then passed it to Mitch.

As Mitch took a hit, Keesha added, "And you need to forget about Halleigh. If Malek goes, then she needs to go. She'll get suspicious, and she'll become a problem if you don't get rid of her up front, so forget about them wet dreams you been having about her."

Keesha walked around and stood in front of Mitch. Her red thong and bra didn't even distract Mitch as he absorbed what she had just said. Keesha walked into the bathroom and out of sight as Mitch continued to get blazed.

Mitch didn't realize it, but the same way he'd attempted to manipulate Halleigh, Keesha had just manipulated him. The only difference was when a woman does things, she does it right.

As Mitch stood there blazing on the blunt, his jealousy for Malek turned to animosity, and he began to formulate a plan to knock him off his throne. It was a tricky situation, trying to get rid of Malek, who had inherited a lot of love and respect off Jamaica Joe's strength. He couldn't just

kill him and then expect the city to pledge their allegiance behind him. There would be uproar, and Malek's loyal soldiers and allies would always have revenge in their hearts. He had to do it quietly and make it look like the work of an outsider. That way, when Malek was out of the picture, everyone would follow Mitch, no questions asked.

Ding-Dong!

Keesha came out of the bathroom with a bandage on her face after hearing the doorbell ring. She was still unclothed, but that didn't seem to matter. She rolled her eyes and said, "I'll get it." Her "fatty" swallowed the thong as she left the room.

Mitch put on a pair of Sean John jeans over the boxers he'd been sporting as he continued to smoke, his chiseled and tattooed upper body still showing.

Keesha appeared in the doorway just as Mitch was about to exit. "Your daddy's here," she said with a condescending look, referring to Malek.

Mitch stroked her burnt cheek and whispered, "You don't learn well, do you?" He gave her a hard pat, making her flinch in pain. "Don't worry. I'll teach you as soon as my company leaves." He smiled as he thought about the foot he would put up her ass later.

Mitch and Keesha had a love-hate relationship at best. They weren't a couple by any means. Sweets had put Keesha on Mitch to make sure that he remembered why Malek had to get "got."

They both knew their relationship was about business, but as soon as Mitch saw Keesha's small waist and fat onion-shaped behind, he pictured himself hitting it. It wasn't long before he actually did. So now they fucked and plotted, plotted and schemed, fucked, plotted, and schemed all day.

Mitch knew she was seeking the grand prize. After he took over, she wanted to be wifey. *Never that*, he thought as he entered his living room and found Malek standing in the doorway. He forced himself to turn his frown into a friendly smile. "Bro, what's good?" he asked, approaching Malek and giving him some dap.

"I've got to talk to you about something," Malek said seriously. He nodded toward the back of the house and added, "In private."

"Yeah, a'ight. Let me grab a shirt and we'll go grab some food or something." Mitch walked away and disappeared into the bedroom.

Malek decided to go wait out in the car for Mitch. He didn't know if it was just his nerves, but Mitch seemed to be taking extra long to come outside. He looked at the time on his cell phone and realized Mitch had kept him waiting for more than fifteen minutes.

When Mitch finally got inside the car, Malek cut him a look but decided against speaking on it. He just started up his ride and pulled away from the curb in silence as soon as Mitch closed his door.

Malek's focus was straight ahead, and he seemed

distant, causing Mitch to be a little uneasy. *I hope he ain't heard nothing about the deal I made with Sweets,* Mitch thought as he shifted in his seat.

All of a sudden, the leather interior of Malek's car felt like hot coals on Mitch's ass, and he began to sweat as the silent seconds ticked by. As Mitch was sweating bullets, Malek was lost in his own thoughts.

Malek knew he couldn't get fifty joints off on his own in three weeks. He would need Mitch's help. Once he made his money, he planned on stepping down and giving it all to Mitch, but he would wait to tell him that news until after his work was already moved. Malek didn't need Mitch thinking for self while pushing his product.

"The duffel bag in the back got fifty in it," Malek stated.

Mitch finally let out a sigh of relief when he realized he wasn't busted. "Fifty? Why so many?" he asked.

"We got some moves we need to make," Malek replied vaguely. "We need to get 'em off in three weeks. You think you can make that happen?" Malek kept his eyes on the road and never even looked over at Mitch.

"I don't see why not," Mitch answered with a shrug. Inside, he couldn't help but wonder what the time frame was all about, why Malek was set on moving the dope so fast.

"Make sure all the spots get hit with double.

All of them niggas need to be on post twenty-four hours. For the next three weeks, ain't no such thing as sleeping. Nobody gets work on consignment. For the loyal niggas that cop from us, lower the price. Tell 'em they can get the bricks for eighteen each, or two for thirty. Make it so they can't tell you no. Get 'em off however you can.

"Be smart, though. We ain't had no trouble from the police so far, and we don't want none now, nah mean?"

"Yeah, I hear you. I got it," Mitch replied, still puzzled by the sudden urgency in moving product. "What's going on? I mean, why is there such a hurry to make this move? What's going on in three weeks?" Mitch chuckled. "You got a ransom you got to pay or something?"

Malek remained serious, acting as if Mitch hadn't even asked him anything. "When they're all done, I'll bless you with something. I'm not gon' be out here like that because Halleigh needs me right now, so I'ma need you to be my eyes, ears, and pistols. You feel me?" Once again he looked over at Mitch.

"I feel you."

"I'm not going hard for nothing, though, bro. It's something in it for everybody. Everybody's gon' eat as long as it gets done," Malek promised as he pulled back onto Mitch's street after circling the block.

"I got you, fam. It's as good as done," Mitch

replied. He frowned when Malek stopped in front of his house. "We ain't going to eat?"

"You got three weeks, baby. Time is money." Malek popped his car locks, signaling for Mitch to exit his vehicle. "We can eat later. Oh and, trust me, we'll eat, but right now, it's all about that paper."

On that note, Mitch exited the car, and was left standing there confused as Malek peeled off.

Chapter Four

Mitch hit the streets with a vengeance all right, but his motivation was greed. By giving Mitch free reign over fifty kilos of cocaine, Malek had given him the push he needed to put his plan into action. Mitch was going to sell the coke, but he had no intention of giving all that paper back to Malek, and he definitely wasn't planning on lowering the prices. There was a cocaine drought in the Midwest, and Mitch was going to take full advantage of it. Supply and demand was the only scale he set his prices to. In fact, he was taxing for the bricks by charging cats twenty-four stacks for just one. Malek's loyal customers were the only ones getting a lowered rate, only so that they wouldn't go back and complain to Malek. Everybody else was getting raped by his outrageous prices.

It was nothing for Mitch to blow through the dope, because he had Sweets on deck for more

than half of them. By the time the three weeks was up, he would be close to a million dollars richer, and Malek would be closer to death.

Mitch, like a lot of other cats in the game, had always been "lightweight" jealous of Malek because of how he seemed to have come up in the game without putting in half as much work as some other cats did. It was as if all he had to do was grow into his inheritance. Mitch didn't care how hard Malek made himself out to be; he wasn't no true hood nigga. It made Mitch sick, especially when he recalled all those write-ups in the local paper about Flint's godson, the kid that was going to put the city on the map the same way LeBron put Cleveland on the map. Now more than ever, Mitch was bound and determined to put his own self on the map.

He used to feel bad and disloyal at the thoughts of undermining Malek that would often cross his mind, but Keesha had kicked her "fuck Malek campaign" into overdrive. That, along with the fact that Mitch was getting crazy paid, helped to erase any guilt that remained. Malek's demise was an equal trade for Mitch's come-up. The day that Malek called to ask for the money would be the same day that he would be found leaking somewhere. There was no way Mitch was letting that much dough slip through his hands.

Malek made it his personal mission to visit Halleigh every day in the hospital. Her room

was filled with flowers and balloons from him, and every day he was bringing her a new gift. He was just so grateful to have her in his life and so excited by the fact that he was about to be a father. The flowers, balloons, and gifts weren't bribes just to get Halleigh to forgive him for the part he played in her being in the hospital in the first place. He truly wanted to give Halleigh the world and show her in every way how much he truly loved her.

Eventually, Halleigh did express her true forgiveness to Malek, although he had not forgiven himself yet. Every time Halleigh smiled at him, he would think of how close he had come to never seeing her smile again.

"I'ma take care of you. You know that, right?" he asked her as he held her hand.

"I know, Malek, but who's going to take care of you?" she countered. "I know you're not going to leave the streets alone."

"I am," he said abruptly and definitively. "By the time you walk out of here, I'll be out of the game."

"Yeah, right, Malek. You're just saying all of that, thinking it will make me feel better, heal better, and get out of here even faster. I don't know. But I do know how addictive the street game is. It's much easier to just say you're going to give it all up than to actually do it. Trust me, I know."

"But I'm serious, Hal. At the end of the day, a nigga's word is really all he got. My word is gold,

it always has been, when it comes to you. You don't know that by now?"

The tone of sincerity in his voice let her know that he wasn't lying.

"I don't want to lose you. If I got to give up the streets to keep you, then that's that. Plus, you being in that rehab center has been eating me alive. I can't believe I did this to you."

Their intimate moment was interrupted by a knock at the door. They both looked up and saw Sharina walk through the door.

Malek stood up to leave so that he could give mother and daughter some privacy. Halleigh hadn't really told him what went down when they met each other at the rehab center, but he knew they must still have a lot to talk about.

Halleigh shook her head and said, "No, Malek, stay."

He sat down reluctantly, but held her hand tightly to give her his support. Seeing Halleigh's mother put a bad taste in Malek's mouth. He didn't have too much respect for her, considering all that she had put the love of his life through.

"You're so pretty," Sharina said almost in a whisper as she slowly crept toward Halleigh's bedside. She stopped before making it all the way over to Halleigh. Her eyes clouded over with tears, almost like she was seeing her daughter for the first time.

Halleigh was silent as she stared at her mother from the hospital bed. There was so much anger built up inside of her. As she looked at her

mother, she tried to forget that it was Sharina's sin that had sent her world spiraling out of control. On that fateful night, Halleigh's life was forever changed for the worse. Looking at Sharina, it was hard not to also see the men she'd let rape her daughter for the sake of a hit.

"It's been a long time, baby girl. You're all grown-up now. You remind me so much of myself." Sharina stood at the foot of the bed nervously twiddling her fingers as she waited for Halleigh to respond. She seemed to be afraid to get too close.

Two years ago, Sharina was frail and sickly-looking; but now, it appeared as though she had picked up some of her weight, and she wasn't high, which made her almost unrecognizable.

"Well, I'm not you. I could never be you," Halleigh shot at her. "Why did you come here?"

"I'm sorry, Halleigh. I'm so sorry. I've thought about you every day since then," Sharina said. She swallowed the knot in her throat, hoping she wouldn't have to elaborate. Her hopes were shattered when Halleigh sat straight up in her bed and spoke.

"Since when, Ma? Since the first time you pawned my Christmas gifts to get high? Since the time we got put out in the streets in the winter because you spent the rent money on dope?"

"I know, baby."

Halleigh almost jumped out of her bed and across the room. "No, you don't know shit! You have no clue what I've been through!"

Growing up, Halleigh had never disrespected her mother. Dopefiend or not, Sharina was her mother, and Halleigh had always treated her as such. But right now, she could no longer control all of the bitterness that had mounted up against her mother. "See, I could've forgiven all of those things, Ma. I didn't want the Christmas gifts. I would have lived in a cardboard box with you. I accepted you for who you were, because you were still my mother and I loved you. You were the only one I had."

"I love you too, baby girl," Sharina pleaded as tears fell down her cheeks.

"No, you don't. I forgave you time and time again, Ma, but you did the unforgivable the day you sold my virginity to the dopeman!"

There, it had been said. Sharina always knew that decision would come back to haunt her someday. What she did to her daughter was the thing she wished she could take back more than anything.

"I know, baby. I have regretted that since the day I did it, baby. I'm so sorry. I truly am. You have to forgive me." Sharina took one step closer to the bed, as if the invisible wall that separated them was slowly being chiseled away. "I'm clean now, Halleigh. I've been clean for six months, baby. I go to meetings at the rehab center to stay clean. I'm going to do it this time, if not for myself, then for you." She looked down at Halleigh's small baby bump. "And it looks like

for my grandbaby too. I just want to be here for you and make it right."

Desperate for her daughter's affection, Sharina was begging like Keith Sweat. She didn't know her daughter had changed, and was no longer the sweet, forgiving, naïve little girl she had somehow managed to raise during her sober moments. Halleigh might not have wished her mother dead in that rehab center shootout, but at the same time, she didn't have much love for her.

"I'm glad you're clean," Halleigh said with a nod before going back to rest in her bed. "Maybe now you're clearheaded enough to think about how you ruined my life." She glared at her mother.

"Do you know the things I've had to do because of you?" Halleigh spat. "You were so used up that you couldn't have paid a corner boy to let you fuck your way into a high, so you sold me. You pimped me out and let them rape me. That was mine to keep and give to who I wanted, but you took it from me!"

Malek could see the past stirring up fresh anger in Halleigh. As he thought about the role Sharina played in robbing him of the precious gift Halleigh had been saving for him, new anger began to rise up in him also. Seeing his baby's mother was getting all "rallied" and stressed, he wanted to tell her to just calm down, even ask her mother to leave the room; but he

knew this moment was a long time coming, and something Halleigh probably needed to let go of. Who was he to stand in her way?

"I can never forgive you for that," Halleigh told Sharina.

Sharina finally realized her daughter wasn't the same anymore. It was evident from the look in her eyes that the streets had injected its DNA into her baby. Now she was as cold as a Michigan winter. "I know it hurts," Sharina cried. "I know I did wrong, but I'm your mother, Halleigh. You're my baby. I need you."

"Well, I don't need a mother. I'm a grown-ass woman now. There's nothing left to raise. The streets raised me, but you know what? You were good for something. You showed me how not to treat my child. So this baby I'm carrying in my stomach is lucky, because I'm determined not to fuck up, just to avoid being like you."

Halleigh's words were so sharp they cut Sharina to the bone. Malek could see her shivering in pain as she began to backpedal out of the room.

"I'm sorry, baby girl. Mama had a monkey on her back. You have to know that I would have never allowed those things to happen to you otherwise. I love you, and I only hope that you will let me back into your life one day so that, even if you don't want me to be a mother to you, I can at least be a grandmother to my grandchild."

"You will never be a part of my baby's life!"

Halleigh said, throwing daggers at her mother's heart. She knew from the look on Sharina's face that she hit the bull's-eye. "We don't need you. Now, please leave."

While spitting those last words at her mother, Halleigh had managed to stay dry-eyed. Any tears she might have shed for her mother in the past were now long gone and long forgotten. Not one teardrop had even threatened to appear in her eyes. She was as cold as ice, her tears frozen solid and unable to form.

Halleigh had chosen her words carefully. They were calculated to inflict as much pain as possible. She knew that no words could ever hurt her mother as much as Sharina had hurt her, but still, it had been well worth the effort.

After speaking her mind, Halleigh had hoped to feel some sense of relief, victory even, but that wasn't the case. Just as soon as Sharina walked out of the room, the ice block around Halleigh's heart quickly melted, and she broke down in tears. She cried the hardest she had ever done in her life, heaving violently as she thought of her rape, of the woman she'd once loved and would have done anything for, and of how proud she truly was that her mother had gotten herself clean. With so many emotions taking over her mind, all Halleigh could do was cry.

Halleigh knew she might never see her mother again after what she'd just said to her, and as much as she hated to admit it, it hurt. No matter how painful that was, though, she couldn't for-

give her. Right now, forgiveness just wasn't in her. How she was even able to forgive Malek was beyond her own understanding. All she knew was that her heart had no more room for mercy. Not right now.

She was just now starting to piece her life back together, and that was only by the grace of God—and Malek's love. She refused to let her mother come and break up her happiness with Malek yet again. Even if her mother was sober now, there was no telling how long that might last. Halleigh didn't have time to let someone else's burdens become her own. She had to let sleeping dogs lie and move on with her life. Logically she knew this, but it didn't ease the pain she felt in her chest as she bawled like a baby.

Malek sat by her side, stroking her hair and rubbing her back, reassuring her that everything would be all right. He'd actually been shocked by how cruelly Halleigh spoke to her mother. Sharina had done the worst thing a mother could do to her daughter, but a part of him still wanted to urge Halleigh toward forgiveness, because he knew what it was like not to have a mother at all.

His mother was gone, and he would do anything to bring her back if he could; life was short and could be taken away at any second. But he didn't force his opinion on Halleigh. Instead, he comforted her in her time of need, trusting her to handle the situation as she saw fit. He knew that she'd gone through some awful things as a

result of her mother—some things that she probably would never even tell him—so he let her scream on her mother, and then comforted her as she cried herself to sleep.

As the cold, icy layer melted away from Halleigh's heart, it seemed to be doing the same for Malek. Perhaps things could go back to the way they were after all . . . just not so easily.

Chapter Five

After spending three weeks in the hospital, Halleigh emerged from the elevator in a wheelchair, which Malek was pushing. He leaned over to kiss her cheek.

"I love you, Halleigh," he said, finally glad that his woman was coming home where she belonged.

"I love you forever, Malek," she responded as he wheeled her through the sliding glass doors to where his car was waiting.

Halleigh grimaced at the pain that shot through her whenever she moved. The doctors had been giving her pain medication throughout her hospital stay, but because she was pregnant, they couldn't give her anything too strong. She had lost a lot of blood when she was shot, and she had dropped a lot of weight, so her doctors were giving her high doses of vitamins to get her energy back to where it should be.

"I'm going to drop you off at home and then go fill your prescriptions," Malek told her as he climbed into the driver's seat and pulled off. "I have to swing by and pick something up from Mitch, too, so I may be gone for a couple hours."

Halleigh looked at Malek through disappointed eyes. In her heart she felt like he would never give up the streets. For the past three weeks, he had been making lifetime promises, assuring her that he was getting out of the game, but something was telling her that he couldn't give it all up, that the hold of the streets was far too strong on him.

She didn't feel sure about how important she was to him, and she needed, more than anything, for him to know she was willing to commit to being a permanent fixture in his life. The game was temporary.

Noticing the look in Halleigh's eyes, Malek told her, "Don't look like that, Hal. I told you I'm through with the streets, and I meant it. All I'm going to do today is pick up my money that I got out there, and then I'm out for good."

Once in front of their spot, he opened his car door and helped Halleigh inside. She was so grateful to walk into her own home after her extended stay in the hospital. She couldn't wait to take a bath, get some real food, and then pass out in her own therapeutic Sleep Number bed. Malek suggested she lay down and get some rest first. He promised that he would help her with a bath once he got back, but she wanted to get

cleaned up to lay in her nice, clean, freshly made bed.

After getting out of the bath and slipping into some comfy pajamas, Halleigh made her way down to the kitchen, where Malek was fixing her something to eat before he headed out. Halleigh noticed a small box tied with a bright red ribbon on the countertop.

"Is that for me?" she asked Malek.

Malek didn't respond as he poured some canned soup into a bowl, but his smile was enough for Halleigh to get excited. She knew it was jewelry because of how small the box was. She walked over to it and shook it playfully before untying the ribbon and opening the box. Inside was a Mercedes key surrounded by red tissue paper.

"I upgraded you, ma. You and my shorty got to ride in the best," Malek said with a wink. He walked over to Halleigh and rubbed her belly.

"Where is it?" she asked excitedly, jumping up and down in spite of her pain.

Malek motioned his head toward the garage, and Halleigh walked slowly through the door. She stopped dead in her tracks when she saw the custom, powder-pink 6 Series. It was just like Malek's, except it was super-feminine. "Oh my God! Malek, I love it, boy!" she screamed in delight as she rushed to admire the white leather interior.

"I thought you might." Malek checked the time on his phone. "Hal, I've got to spin the

block for a minute. I'll be back before it gets too late, a'ight."

"Yeah, yeah, okay," she said distractedly as she messed with the gadgets on the inside.

Malek laughed. "Your soup is inside on the counter. Don't let it get cold."

Still, Halleigh paid him little attention.

"Call me if you need me," he said as he headed off to take care of his final business transactions on the streets.

When Mitch received the call from Malek asking him to meet up, he knew it was time. He'd been watching his calendar and counting down to the day when the streets would be his. He had easily blown through the weight Malek hit him with, partly because he had supplied Sweets with a "butter" price. Malek didn't know his dope was going to his adversary, but after today, it wouldn't matter anyway. He would be a distant memory.

Mitch grabbed the two duffel bags full of money and the twin pistols for security. The bags were filled to capacity with all street cash, the bills dirty and crinkled. Dirty money. He laughed at how paid he actually was. It felt good to have so much money. He was on cloud nine, and on his way to get rid of the only person who could possibly bring him down from his high.

He made sure both of his chrome 9 "milli's" were off safety then stuffed them into his shoulder holsters, one tucked safely between each arm. He put on his black leather Pelle Pelle coat, which concealed the holster, and then went to meet Malek.

Malek had been waiting at his spare apartment for Mitch to arrive. He'd rented the apartment just to have an extra place to rest his head, but since he and Halleigh had started a life together, he rarely used it. It was convenient for the purpose he was using it for tonight.

When Malek called, Mitch had assured him that all of the coke was gone and they were sitting on a gold mine. One million dollars was a lot of money—more money than a lot of people saw in their entire lives. Malek had always been smart, and watching Jamaica Joe as he reigned supreme only helped him to perfect his own hustle. He had a nice chunk of change saved up already, and with the money Mitch was about to deliver, it would be more than enough for him and Halleigh to relocate and start fresh.

He wasn't no dummy, though. He knew he couldn't just let that money sit idle when it could be making him more. The only difference was it would be legal this time. He really wanted to link up with a financial advisor because he wanted to make some arrangements for Halleigh

and his baby. Just in case anything ever happened to him, he wanted them to be set for life.

When Malek heard the knock at the door, he knew it was Mitch. He was the only other person who knew about the apartment. Malek didn't bother to check the peephole. He opened the door to find Mitch standing at his doorway.

"What's good, bro?" Malek asked. "Come on in." He stepped aside for Mitch to enter.

Mitch came in and looked around. Malek didn't notice the paranoia in his eyes because he was too busy thinking about getting paid.

"You got the bread, fam?" Malek asked, rubbing his hands together.

Mitch lifted the duffel bag.

"Nigga, what's good? You all silent and shit," Malek commented as he motioned toward his sectional sofa. "Have a seat. There's something important I need to holla at you about."

Mitch made sure he kept the duffel bag near his feet and then took a seat on the couch. He could hear his heart beating rapidly in his ear as Malek walked over to the bar. Mitch knew this was his chance to do what he'd really come to do. Malek's back was toward him, so he could easily shoot him from behind and dip without looking back.

Mitch reached inside his jacket to retrieve one of his guns, but halted when Malek said, "I'm getting out the game, Mitch."

Mitch released the grip on his steel. "What you mean, out the game?"

Malek finally turned to stare Mitch in the eyes as he spoke. "I mean I'm through. Halleigh is pregnant with my baby, and I'm trying to be around to raise him and see him grow. I don't want to make my wife bury me the way Joe did with Kim. That's why I needed that weight moved so quickly. The day Hal walked out of the hospital, I promised her I would walk away from the streets."

"And that day is today?" Mitch questioned. He had to see what Malek intended for him, because if he thought he was taking all the money and leaving Mitch with nothing, then Mitch still planned on putting two in Malek and taking the cash to build an empire of his own. But before he moved forward with his plan, he decided to give Malek the benefit of the doubt and hear him out.

"That's right. I appreciate you, fam. You've been loyal since we decided to do this together, and now I've got to hand it all down to you, bro. The money you made off of them bricks, two-fifty of it is yours, man, to cop your own weight and do your own thing. I'll even plug you in with my connect. I got the connect from Joe.

"It's all love, baby, but I've got to get out while I still have air in my lungs."

Mitch smiled deviously and replied, "No doubt, baby. You definitely got an angel watching over you, fam. You've dodged a lot of bullets. You're a smart man." He couldn't help but chuckle inside at his personal joke. Malek had dodged bul-

lets all right. Unknowingly, he'd just dodged two.

Mitch was satisfied with Malek's severance pay, and decided to kill his plan instead of his boy. Two hundred and fifty thousand dollars was enough cake to get up and running and stash some for a rainy day. If Malek was getting out of the game anyway, then he wouldn't be a problem to Sweets or anyone else, so the situation was fitting for everyone. How Mitch saw it, it was a win-win situation for every player.

"So I take it you good with that, fam?" Malek walked over to Mitch with two shots of liquor in hand and extended one to him.

A smile crossed Mitch's lips as he accepted the shot. "It's all good."

"It's been a short run, but a good run," Malek said as he held out his glass.

Mitch did the same and they clinked their classes together and then downed the liquor in one swallow.

"Now, let's count this money so I can get back to wifey." Malek headed back to the kitchen, nodding for Mitch to follow. Mitch grabbed the bags and did just that.

Malek went to his refrigerator and grabbed two Coronas out and tossed one to Mitch, who then poured all of the money onto the table. They sat down and went to work counting and dividing the money.

"Congrats on your family, man," Mitch stated,

like he had never had larcenous thoughts on his mind.

"Thanks, my nigga. I'm about to take this money and take care of her, bro. She deserves it."

"That she does," Mitch replied. "That she does."

Chapter Six

After counting out all of the money and breaking Mitch off with a hefty percentage, Malek had $750,000 in the trunk of his car. He was overjoyed at the fact that he could now live comfortably with his lady for years to come. He still had $500,000 saved up from the money Jamaica Joe had left him, so he was indeed a millionaire, with a little bit of change to spare.

He'd lost track of time, sharing last drinks and thoughts with Mitch. He punched eighty on the speedometer, until finally he was sitting in the driveway at his home. He jumped out of the car in excitement, grabbed the duffel bags out of the trunk, and hauled them into the house.

"Halleigh!" he yelled as soon as he entered. He didn't care that it was three o'clock in the morning. He couldn't contain his excitement and wanted to share his departure from the

game with her. He couldn't wait to let her know it was real, that he was truly a man of his word.

"Hal!"

"Malek, what's wrong?" she asked sleepily as she came out of the bedroom. "Why are you yelling?"

"This is why, Hal"—He emptied the contents of one of the duffel bags all over the floor.

Halleigh wasn't the least bit excited, and once again, a look of disappointment showed on her face. "I've seen your re-up money before, Malek." She shook her head and then flailed her arms in defeat. "I thought we had an agreement that you were out of the game?" Hal asked, not out of anger but confusion. She really didn't want to see Malek get hurt or lose his life the way so many hustlers before him had done.

"This ain't re-up paper, baby girl. It's ours. All of this money belongs to us, and I'm going to spoil you and my seed for the rest of my life." Malek rushed toward the love of his life and scooped her in his arms.

Consumed with so much happiness, Halleigh didn't even flinch at the pain she was in as she wrapped her legs around Malek's waist and he held her securely under her bottom. He spun her around and kissed her passionately.

"I need a vacation," Malek said, imitating the popular rap song by Young Jeezy.

Halleigh laughed as Malek laid her down gently on the money-littered floor.

"We can go wherever you like, Halleigh. Just pick a place and we're out."

"I really just want to get out of Flint. That's all I've ever wanted from day one," Halleigh confessed. "Our history here ain't all that great. I just want to go somewhere and start over. Maybe even go back to school or something. I don't really even have to be far from here. Let's go to Detroit or Saginaw, just anywhere but here."

Saginaw and Detroit were just as ruthless and hood as Flint, but the way Halleigh spoke of them, one would have thought she was talking about going to Paris.

"I don't know, Hal. That's just a different hood, same shit. I wanna take you to the Bahamas or something, so we can live like rich niggas do."

Halleigh laughed at Malek's crass outlook on the world. "I don't care about being in the hood, Malek. I just don't want to be in Flint. At least in Saginaw no one will know us. We'll be regular just like everybody else. And since you wanna see how rich niggas live, you can take me on a vacation. We'll go to an island in the Caribbean."

Malek kissed Halleigh gently and replied, "Okay, ma, whatever you want. You handle the passports and everything. The money will be in the safe. You know the combination. My money is your money. Take care of everything and make arrangements for us to leave Flint when we get back from our vacation. Deal?"

Halleigh smiled. "Deal." She couldn't believe it was happening, that she was finally getting out of Flint once and for all. And, God willing, she was never coming back.

Halleigh handled all of the details regarding their trip and their permanent relocation after their return. She had decided that they would move to Saginaw, a small city about a half-hour north of Flint. She decided against Detroit because, in her days as a Manolo Mami, many of her clients had been ballers from the D, and she didn't want to run into anyone who might remember her from her former occupation. She was trying to let her past go and focus on the present, and at the rate she had been turning tricks for Manolo, she knew if she and Malek moved to Detroit, she would inevitably run into someone she used to do business with.

She was also excited about her pregnancy. She was healing well from her gunshot wound. Fortunately for her, it was only a flesh wound, and although the bullet had been the greatest pain she ever felt, it hadn't hit any major arteries or organs. The doctors told her that ordinarily she wouldn't have been in the hospital for more than a week, but with her pregnancy and all, they didn't want to take any chances. She was very grateful to be alive, and she thanked God for the safety of her baby as well.

She booked an all-inclusive trip to the Turks and Caicos Islands and filled out expedited paperwork for passports for herself and Malek. They were scheduled to leave in two weeks, which gave her more than enough time to secure a place to live in Saginaw and move most of their things from their home in Flint. She didn't want to rush into purchasing another home, so she decided to lease a condominium and wait for their home in Flint to be sold first.

She didn't see Malek much in the two weeks prior to their trip, since she was always on the go, taking care of their trip, and he was always asleep, catching up on years of missed sleep from hustling. She didn't mind him taking time to rest. She figured his mind and body needed it after the non-stop hustle he'd been on ever since blowing his NBA shot. Malek had chosen a hard path all because of his love for her, and she appreciated him for it.

A part of her felt guilty because she knew, had it not been for her, Malek would never have committed that robbery. He'd be living out his dreams in the NBA. For that sacrifice, she promised herself that she would always make him happy. That was one of the reasons why she had decided to forgive him. That, and the fact that he was her soul mate and had proven himself time and time again to her. She didn't care how corny it sounded. The child in her stomach linked them together for a lifetime. She was beginning to re-

alize that their relationship was bigger than the two of them. They were now a family.

Halleigh made it her personal mission in life to be there for Malek the way he'd always been there for her. As she thought about how much she loved him, she began to grow more and more excited about their vacation to the Turks and Caicos. She had been fantasizing about going to the burgeoning tourist location ever since she'd learned of LisaRaye marrying the island's premier. Fuck the Bahamas. If a black person owned the island, that's where she wanted to be.

Malek was all she needed, and just the fact that they would be off in some exotic place, secluded from everything else in the world, made her smile. She couldn't wait to have her man all to herself.

A sexy smile graced her lips as she hit a U-turn in the middle of the street. *I've got to hit up Vickie's Secret because on this trip, I'm going to show Malek exactly how much I love him—all day and all night.*

Chapter Seven

Halleigh shook her head and giggled while listening to Malek snore. They had been on the plane for five hours, and Malek had been knocked out since he first sat down. Halleigh, on the other hand, was too geeked to sleep. She could already see the crystal-clear ocean water and sandy-white beaches. She could hardly contain her excitement as she gripped Malek's hand tightly and did everything in her power to wake him up without getting him upset.

She coughed loudly, but he didn't stir, which only irritated her. She turned on his overhead reading light, hoping it would shine in his face and cause him to awaken. Again, no response. She knew she was being selfish, but she needed someone to talk to. She sighed loudly and removed her hand from his to lean against the window.

The feeling of Halleigh pulling away from him

finally made Malek open his eyes. Holding on to her hand had comforted him and put his mind at ease enough for him to close his eyes. As soon as he felt his connection to her cease, he instantly awoke.

"What's good, ma? How long we been in the air?" he asked as he rubbed the sleep out of his eyes.

"Five hours, and you've been sleeping the whole time," Halleigh said with an eye roll.

Malek laughed and replied, "I felt you trying to wake me up, with your big-head ass."

Halleigh smiled and punched his arm gently. "Shut up. I was bored. Our vacation started the moment we arrived at the airport, not when we land."

"Okay, okay, you big baby. I'm all yours for the rest of the trip, and I'll make sure you have a good time." Malek leaned over and whispered in her ear, "Meet me in the bathroom in a couple minutes so I can really show you that our vacation has officially started."

Halleigh gave Malek a mischievous grin and nodded her head as she watched him get up and make his way down the narrow aisle to the bathroom in the back of the plane. A normal chick might have been nervous, but Halleigh lived for moments like this. She loved sex—not tricking and sex with random men, but sex with Malek. Since the first time he touched her, she had become addicted to him, and he could get it whenever, wherever.

She waited for just a couple of minutes and looked around the aircraft discreetly to make sure no one was watching her. After she was comfortable that no one was focused on her, she got up with her purse in hand and walked to the bathroom. When she got there, she could see where Malek had left the door just barely open for her. She quickly snuck inside and closed the door behind her. She slid the lock, causing the *occupied* light come on in the cabin of the plane.

There Malek stood, pants down, and a huge smile on his face.

"You are so bad," she whispered to him.

Not in the mood for words, Malek turned her around and kissed her hungrily while his hands grabbed her behind. He pressed his groin against hers to show her how hard he was. He felt like he was getting ready to burst through the fabric of his Nike sweats. His hands moved quickly and with expertise as he unbuttoned her skintight jeans. He knew she didn't have on panties. She never wore them, which only aroused him more. He lifted her up and put her on the tiny sink.

"Malek, this sink is going to break." Her protest was soon followed by a moan, as her man cupped her breasts.

"Shh," he whispered. He got down on his knees, spread her thighs, and dove into her wet pussy. He knew oral sex was her weakness.

Halleigh's head fell back in pleasure, and she closed her eyes as soon as Malek's tongue hit her

pulsating clit. She began to grind her hips slowly, making love to his face.

"Ooh shit, Malek," she moaned. "Yes, daddy, eat this pussy."

Malek took orders very well and devoured her as he began to stroke himself into pleasure.

"Malek, I'm cumming," she whispered.

"I know," he replied as he continued to feast.

Halleigh trembled as her love came down. Malek arose then sat on the toilet, his dick sticking straight in the air. Halleigh hopped off the sink and rode Malek backward. She would never allow herself to orgasm without pleasing him as well. She grinded her ass into his groin, and within two minutes, Malek was cumming inside of her.

Receiving double the pleasure, Halleigh felt another orgasm coming on, so she sped up the process by putting her fingers on her pussy and stimulating her clit into bliss. The rendezvous lasted only a few minutes, but it was some of the best sex they'd ever had.

Malek wiped his face, rinsed his mouth with a travel-sized mouthwash that Halleigh had in her purse, and then kissed her lips before exiting the bathroom. He ran straight into a flight attendant who was standing there with her arms folded and an accusatory expression on her face.

"Excuse me, miss," Malek said smoothly. "Do you have any Vernors and crackers for my sister, or anything that may settle her stomach? She's

pregnant and has been throwing up in this bath-room for the past fifteen minutes."

The flight attendant immediately wiped the angry look off her face and replaced it with a concerned one. "Oh, of course, sir. I was just going to knock to see if you needed any assistance. Only one passenger at a time is allowed in the bath-room, but under the circumstances, I understand."

Overhearing the conversation outside the door, Halleigh smiled at Malek's wit and then leaned over the toilet as if she was going to heave. Before exiting the restroom, she sprayed two splashes of body spray to erase the smell of sex and then proceeded to her seat, her hand over her stomach.

The flight attendant delivered the crackers and pop to Halleigh, who smiled graciously, still feigning nausea.

Halleigh flashed Malek a devilish smile and leaned back in the comfortable first-class seat. All it took was some good sex to put her to sleep. She closed her eyes and invited the darkness that took her under as Malek gripped her hand.

"I love you, Hal," were the last words she heard Malek whisper into her ear.

Chapter Eight

The island was even more beautiful than either of them could have imagined. Coming up in a concrete jungle, neither of them ever thought they would see a place so grand. All they knew was what was presented to them growing up, which was death, destruction, and poverty. Everyone Halleigh knew was dead broke and robbing Peter to pay Paul. It was just a way of life for the folks of Flint, Michigan. It was a city of little hope, and according to many statistics, a dead city.

This is how I'm supposed to live, Halleigh thought as she followed Malek into their resort. She looked around the luxurious place in awe, feeling like a kid in a candy store. "We're a long way from the ghetto," she said to Malek with a warm smile.

"Yeah, we are. I ain't never seen nothing like

this," Malek admitted, as he too seemed to be out of his element.

As he looked around, he noticed some of the other patrons. Everything was so over-the-top—men wearing linen suits and women clad in designer swimsuits, not the trashy show-everything type of bikinis, either. These women could give Naomi, Tyra, and Giselle a run for their money.

All of a sudden, Malek felt insecure in his own skin, as if he were underdressed. He'd wanted to see what it was like to be amongst the rich and the famous. Well, now he was experiencing it firsthand. Hopefully he'd soon adapt.

The couple checked into their beachside villa where they were greeted by their personal concierge. When they finally settled in, they remained silent, still absorbing the entire experience.

Malek finally broke the silence. "Damn, Hal! This is it, ma. We got a butler and everything."

Halleigh stuck up her nose haughtily. "You mean a concierge, good sir," she said in a horrible British accent. She burst out laughing, and Malek hit her with one of the luxury pillows that decorated the bed. He tackled her onto the bed, and she grimaced in pain. "Ow, Malek! Wait a minute," she said as she sat up and examined the scar from her gunshot wound.

"I'm sorry, Hal. I'ma make it up to you."

Halleigh smiled and replied, "Look around us, Malek. You already have." She leaned in toward him and kissed the back of his neck. "Now, let's get out of this room and hit the beach."

Malek frowned. "Hal, we just got off a six-hour flight. Can't we just get some rest tonight and start our day tomorrow? We're here for an entire week."

"Malek, one thing I've learned by being out in the streets is that tomorrow may never come. I live my life for today." She took his hand and placed it on her pregnant stomach. "We live for today."

Malek was extremely tired, but he knew Halleigh was right. Tomorrow was promised to no man. He nodded and said, "A'ight, let's live, ma."

Although most of the day was behind them, the couple enjoyed the rest of the evening together by taking a walk on the resort's private beach. They took the time to pay attention to the sunset for the first time and actually relaxed for a change. They lay on the beach, close to the water, and let the tide wash in on their legs as they talked.

They both felt brand-new, like they were in a whole other world. Flint bred a city of killers and shysters. Everyone who lived there seemed to carry the weight of the world on his shoulders, and had a swagger unlike any other region. "Fuck those who aren't like me and hate those who are" seemed to be the mentality of the entire city. With this attitude came misery, however, and it bred violence and anger.

In their hometown, the couple was always looking over their shoulders and watching their

backs; in fact, the whole city was paranoid. But on the Turks and Caicos Islands, they were able to let go of all that. There were no rules, and for the first time ever in their lives, they felt able to breathe. It was even better because they were able to experience it with each other.

Malek caressed his woman, enjoying every single second that passed.

"I'm sorry. I fucked up, Hal," Malek said as he stared off. "We were supposed to be living like this a long time ago. You weren't supposed to go through what you did."

Halleigh sat up and turned to look at him. "We should leave everything here on this island, Malek—all of our baggage and anger and sadness. I know I've built a lot of that shit up over the years. I'm ready to let it go. I have you now. I have our baby. What else is there? I want for nothing, Malek, and it's not about the money. I just feel complete and safe. I have never been this secure in my life. I don't ever want to lose you."

"And you never will, Hal." Malek placed a soft kiss on her lips.

That ended their conversation, but they said so much more with their bodies. They made love right there on the beach until it was too dark for either of them to see.

Malek carried Halleigh up to their villa and watched her sleep. He wished his mother had lived long enough to really get to know Halleigh.

She was the total opposite of what his mother had made her out to be—just another gold digger chick after his NBA money. Halleigh truly was the one person in his life who he would die for. She was his confidante above all else, and before he went to sleep, he sent a prayer up to God, thanking Him for bringing her to him.

Halleigh and Malek slept well into the afternoon. The 1,000 thread count linens felt like a personal masseuse and just would not let either of them wake up from their peaceful slumber. When they finally awakened, they were well rested and ready to tackle another day.

"What do you want to do today, ma? It's all on you," Malek said as he removed his clothing and prepared to take a shower. He wrapped the plush white towel around his lean waist. He still had the body of a basketball player. Tall and toned, he was perfect in Halleigh's eyes.

"Glass-bottom boat," Halleigh replied excitedly as she jumped out of the bed.

Malek nodded his head. He wasn't much of a water person, not that he knew many black folks from the hood who were, but he had promised Halleigh her heart's desires while on this trip, and he wasn't going to let her down. "Glass-bottom boat it is," he said and then went into the bathroom to shower. He yelled, "Hal, get

some money out of the lining of my suitcase. After you get ready and dressed, we'll dip."

"Okay. And I'll call the front desk to make sure we don't need an appointment or anything. If we do, we can just grab a bite of something to eat first."

Halleigh headed over to Malek's suitcase. She was surprised at the amount of money he had brought with him. He probably had $100,000 stashed in there. She took the money stacks out of the suitcase and put them in the villa safe, taking out a few thousand for the day. Then she locked the safe and proceeded to contact the front desk. She was relieved to find that they didn't need an appointment, but the glass-bottom boat ride was on a first-come first-served basis. The front desk clerk informed her of the departure times.

Halleigh rushed to get ready. She didn't want to miss the next boat, which would be leaving in an hour.

"Mind if I join you?" she asked after removing her clothes and creeping into the bathroom to join her man in the shower.

"Do you really even have to ask?" Malek looked over at Halleigh's naked body. "I thought for sure that you'd had enough last night." He licked his lips. "But you know me . . . always ready to make things happen." He reached out and helped Halleigh into the shower.

"Don't get any ideas, mister." Halleigh play-fully smacked Malek's hands. "Although I could

never get enough of you, we have a boat to catch. It leaves in an hour. I'm only showering with you to save time. So here." She handed Malek a rag. "Get to washing my back, will you?" She winked and smiled at her man then turned her back to him.

"Oh, so it's like that? You just using a brother for convenience?"

"Hmmm . . . something like that." She handed him the bar of soap.

Malek wet Halleigh's rag then lathered it up with soap. Just touching her was turning him on, and his manhood stiffened. "Not even just a quickie?" he whispered into Halleigh's ear, brushing his lips against it.

Malek's soft breath blowing into her ear and just the mere touch of his lips sent chills through Halleigh's body. "Ummmm," she moaned. "Just a quickie, did you say?"

"Yeah, in and out. Nobody gets hurt." By now Malek had dropped both the soap and the rag and was rubbing his hands down Halleigh's sides.

Halleigh abruptly turned to face him. "Make it quick, daddy," she said, throwing her leg up around his waist. "We got a boat to catch."

Almost an hour later, Halleigh and Malek were running down the pier. The quickie had turned out not to be so quick after all.

"Wait!" Halleigh yelled as she ran toward the departing boat. "We're coming!"

The dock person held the boat for Halleigh

and Malek. Halleigh smiled excitedly and boarded the boat first.

Malek, still on the dock, pulled out a wad of money and asked, "How much, my man?"

"We don't accept cash, sir," the attendant said.

"What? What do you mean, you don't accept cash? You don't accept American money or something?"

"You have to go back to the resort and set up an account," the man replied. "All excursion payments must be made at the front desk."

"But we'll miss the boat!" Halleigh exclaimed, wondering why the clerk she had spoken to didn't tell her that when she was on the phone earlier. "Can't you just accept cash this one time? It all spends the same."

"I'm sorry, miss. I will lose my job," the guy stated. "We are not allowed to accept any cash from guests. I would if I could, but it's grounds for immediate termination, whether you really turn in the money or not."

A man who happened to be passing by stopped and interjected, "It's okay. You can charge their boat passes on my account card." He was a blond-haired, blue-eyed man with a tan that looked like it was designed specially by God. He wore Dolce & Gabbana linen pants and a shirt with sandals.

He smiled at Halleigh. "Sounds like the lady here really wants to go on this boat ride." Still

smiling, he looked at Malek. "Gotta give the ladies what they want."

"Thanks! We'll pay you the money," Halleigh said excitedly as Malek stepped onto the boat.

Malek immediately began to count out the bills to hand over to the kind stranger.

The white man shook his head. "No need. I have a house on the island. I'm a regular here, so I have a lot of resort credit," he assured them with the wave of his hand. "Don't worry about it."

Malek shook his head. "No, we'll pay you for it." If he hadn't learned anything else on the streets, he'd learned that everything came with a price. He'd always found it better to set his own price and pay it up front rather than receive the bill later with a much higher price than he'd been willing to pay.

Malek peeled off the exact amount of the boat ride plus an extra fifty for the man's trouble—sort of a convenience fee for him and Halleigh. He handed it to the man.

The guy smiled and nodded. "Okay, I understand. I like a man that pays his own way." He called a ship worker over and handed him the money Malek had just given him. "Bring us a bottle of your finest champagne, and please bring me and my guests menus up to the promenade."

"Right away, sir," the ship worker replied and then disappeared.

Malek watched the man give away the money as if it wasn't shit. *Back home, that would've paid somebody's rent,* he thought.

"I'm Gary, by the way," the man said as he extended his hand to Malek.

Malek shook his hand and introduced himself.

"I'm Halleigh."

The man took Halleigh's hand and planted a light kiss on the back of it. "Nice to meet you, Halleigh."

At first, Malek thought dude might be trying to disrespect him, you know, steal on his girl right in his face like he wasn't nothing, but then he had a change of heart when a gorgeous woman came up and stood next to the man. Her hair was blowing in the wind, and she wore huge designer shades on her face.

Halleigh admired the way the woman walked. She looked like one of the print models in a high-fashion magazine.

"Hey, I thought you forgot about me," the woman said to Gary, not even noticing the couple that stood with him.

"Um, Marie, I want you to meet Halleigh and Malek," Gary said. "They were having a little bit of trouble boarding. I've arranged for us to have drinks and lunch on the promenade deck."

"Well, it's nice to meet you both," she said with a nod. She rested her arms on Gary's shoulders, not bothering to extend them to shake either Halleigh's or Malek's hand. "Shall we?" she

said. Then she led the way to the promenade deck.

Halleigh looked at Malek and made a face that let him know she was impressed with the lady's elegance. They were definitely out of their league, but each was carefully taking note of how Gary and Marie carried themselves.

The young couple from Flint didn't know that only the richest of the rich frequented the Turks, but they'd made up their minds that by the time they revisited the island, they'd fit right in.

When they arrived at their table, Gary asked, "So, Malek, where are you guys from?"

"Flint. Flint, Michigan," he answered. "What about you and your wife?"

"Well, Marie is not my wife, she's the mistress." Gary said it like having a mistress on the side was a normal practice to just flaunt. Perhaps that was true where Gary came from, but in the hood, it was grounds for a nigga to get cut.

Gary kissed Marie's cheek. She appeared proud to bear the title of "Gary's mistress."

Noticing Halleigh's expression of surprise, Marie spoke up. "Oh no, sweetheart, don't look like that," she said to Halleigh in a comforting tone. "I'm not the mistress because I have to be. I'm the mistress because I *choose* to be." She looked over at Gary. "Isn't that right, love?"

Gary nodded in agreement, and then Marie turned her attention back to Halleigh. "You see, Gary's wife gets to play Susie Homemaker while

I fly around the world, shop mercilessly, and fuck the shit out of her husband. I play my position very well," she stated with an arrogant yet confident smile.

Halleigh's eyebrows rose in amazement. She looked at Malek, who sat smiling. "Don't even think about it," she warned him playfully.

Gary laughed. "He wouldn't dare. I wouldn't need a mistress if my wife was as beautiful as you, Halleigh. You're a lucky man, Malek." He held up his champagne flute, and the rest of the group raised theirs as well before taking a sip.

"Halleigh, you are just glowing. How far along are you?" Marie asked.

Halleigh blushed and then removed some of the hair from her face. "Oh . . . um, I'm three months. I didn't know I was showing yet. Most people don't even notice." Halleigh looked down at her champagne glass, wondering if Marie was trying to be funny by asking her about her pregnancy. She began to feel a little guilty.

"Oh, not to worry," Marie said, noticing the look on Halleigh's face. "I'm sure a little sip of champagne won't hurt for now. But, remember, you got a little one in there to look out for."

"Yes, ma'am," Halleigh said, feeling strangely as though Marie was more like a mother figure.

"*Marie* will be fine. Save the 'ma'am' stuff for your elders." Marie winked and then took another sip of her champagne. "Besides, I can barely tell you're pregnant. You have a tiny baby

bump, but your skin and hair are shining with only the vitamins that children can produce."

"You have kids?" Halleigh asked.

"Oh God, no!" Marie downed some more champagne. "I'm not the motherly type, if you know what I mean. I always get jealous when I see what pregnancy does to your complexion, hair, and nails, though. It's like the perfect tan. It's gorgeous. Still, I don't envy mothers the least bit when I see what pregnancy does to their figures. But you look as though you are going to carry yours well."

Halleigh couldn't help but laugh at how shallow the girl was. "Thank you, Marie," she managed to say between chuckles.

"So, where did you say you were from?" Malek asked Gary.

"Miami, but I have a home here as well. I try to visit as much as I can. It's really beautiful here." Gary leaned back and looked out over the water for a minute, then said, "If you guys aren't busy tonight, you're more than welcome to come and join us for dinner. There's this cultural tribe coming to play music for me at my home. You'll love it. You'll get to see and hear some real Caicos flavor," he explained with a charming smile. "What do you say? Does it sound like something you'd be interested in?"

"Of course they are," Marie stated, answering on their behalf. "It'll be fun. I'm glad we met some friends on this island who aren't ancient."

"I'll toast to that." Gary smiled and lifted his glass yet again as they drank to the newfound friendship.

The foursome really became glued at the hip for the remainder of the boat ride. They explored the entire ship, spending most of their time on the bottom of the boat watching the tropical fish through the clear bottom. The couples literally had nothing in common, but that's what made their interaction refreshing.

Halleigh was proud of Malek for holding his own in his conversation with Gary. She noticed that Gary never spoke over Malek's head, and that Malek was speaking politics with Gary as if he had studied it like a science. Malek and Halleigh felt like they were entering high society.

Chapter Nine

Malek and Halleigh took Gary and Marie up on their offer and joined them for dinner. Upon entering Gary's home they were practically speechless.

"Oh my God! This is so unreal. Your home is crazy." Halleigh admired the high vaulted ceiling entryway and marble-lined foyer. Entering the home was like entering paradise, its light-colored décor giving the effect of an indoor beachfront.

Gary laughed at her description and replied, "I hope that's a good thing."

"It is," she answered.

"Well, I want you and Malek to make yourselves at home for the remainder of your stay here. If you'd like, you can check out of the resort and stay here. There's plenty of room. The guest wing is like having your very own private quarters. Trust me, you won't be in our way. In

addition, staying here will save you the cost of paying for a villa."

Halleigh and Malek looked at each other. It was a wonderful offer, and Gary's home made their villa look like something out of the projects, but they didn't want to impose.

Taking note of their hesitance, Gary said, "I have more than enough room here, and the resort allows me to access all of the amenities. Like I said, it's everything staying over at your villa has to offer and more."

"No, we can't, but thanks anyway, man," Malek decided.

"*No?* That's a word I haven't heard in quite some time," Gary said as he walked over to his white leather bar with a glass top and poured two glasses of cognac. "Malek, the first rule to getting rich is learning when you're getting a great deal, and now is one of those times. Come on. It'll be fun."

"Yeah, Halleigh, you guys might as well stay put here. That way Gary and Malek can talk business while you and I take care of business."

Halleigh looked at Marie with a puzzled expression.

"Shopping, sweetheart," Marie told her. "You and I have a lot of shopping to do."

Halleigh turned to Malek skeptically and asked, "Should we?"

Gary walked over to Malek and handed him one of the glasses with the dark liquor. "Of course you should. The bedrooms are upstairs."

Gary motioned his head toward the spiral staircase, which was covered with thick white carpet. "Like I said, make yourselves at home."

Malek finally nodded and shook hands with Gary. "Okay, I appreciate it, man."

"Fine. I'll call over to the resort and have someone pack up all of your things and bring them here. I'll also make sure you receive full credit for the unused portion of your stay."

"There, then it's all settled," Marie said. "Let me show you where you'll be staying."

Marie led Halleigh up the stairs to their deluxe guest quarters, while the men remained downstairs and drank up.

The couples enjoyed their cultural evening with the local band and danced the night away, just the four of them. Malek didn't really dance, but he watched Halleigh have a good time, and enjoyed sipping on the fine liquor.

Later that night, Malek and Halleigh held each other in their bed as they stared out of the open balcony window into the moonlight.

"Today was amazing, Malek," Halleigh said. "Marie and Gary are really cool. I'm so glad we agreed to stay here. And I can't believe the resort agreed to refund all of our money for the room," she added, amazed by the amount of pull Gary had on the island.

"I know, Hal. This is all more than I could have ever imagined, and you deserve it."

"No, Malek," Halleigh corrected him. "*We* deserve it."

Smiling down at his woman, Malek agreed. "You're right. We deserve it. Now get some sleep, ma. I love you."

"I love you forever, Malek."

They dozed off to the sounds of the waves hitting the shore beneath them.

Over the next few days, the couples did everything together, including gambling, sightseeing, and shopping. They dined in the finest restaurants and shopped in designer boutiques, some of which Halleigh had never even heard of. Gary took them to his office in the Turks and showed them where he worked. From the look of the expensive office building and the ministaff he had, Malek could tell Gary was a man of importance. He was intelligent, and was an excellent people person.

Malek was even more surprised to find that Gary was a high school dropout. Here this man had never even finished high school, let alone graduated college, and he was obviously a multimillionaire. To Malek, Gary was hope personified. He was evidence that a man could reach any heights he wanted to, no matter what odds were stacked against him. Malek couldn't wait to get to that level of professionalism. Once he was so far removed from the streets where he couldn't remember what gunpowder and crack cocaine smelled like, like Biggie Smalls said, "Sky was the limit."

On their fourth night together, Malek finally asked Gary something he'd been wondering all along. "How did you get all of this, fam? You seem to be pretty young to be this rich and successful. Your parents put you on or something?"

Gary had never volunteered just what type of work he did, and Malek had never asked, but now curiosity finally got the better of him. He had to know what it would take to reach this level of wealth, and whether he had enough money on reserve to invest in such endeavors.

The ladies were gone out to dinner, so it was only Gary and Malek in the house. They were in the private theater watching an old Al Pacino movie, and Malek hoped that asking Gary about his profession with just the two of them present would make him more apt to share the secret to his fortune.

"I don't mind sharing at all," Gary answered. "I grew up in a trailer park. Everything I have, I got through hard work and making the right connections."

Gary paused for a minute and stared at Malek. Then he added, "Let me ask you a question, Malek. Do you have any credit cards, any 401(k)'s set up? A house? Don't mistake me. I know you are not stupid or broke, so please don't be insulted. I'm just saying I've seen you pull out wads of money all day, which leads me to believe that you are in a business that has no future."

Malek's silence confirmed Gary's suspicions.

"Don't get me wrong, Malek, nor be offended, my friend. That trade you're dabbling in is a gold mine, but you have a girl and baby to think of. You say you're trying to get money like this? Then you have to allow your money to make money. I made my first million through connections and investments."

Malek nodded in agreement. "I hear you, G," Malek said, using the name he'd penned Gary with over the last couple of days. "I had this local lawyer working on my financials, but he couldn't handle the amount of paper I was bringing to him. Then he got greedy and wanted to dip into the cookie jar, so I just said, 'Fuck it! I got a brain and two hands. I can count all this money myself.' Nah mean?"

"I hear you, Malek." Gary nodded.

"How can I get my paper up like this?" Malek looked around Gary's house, admiring all of the expensive furnishings. "I mean, look at all the nice shit you have. I want a piece of this pie."

Malek appreciated Gary taking the time to talk to him. He knew businessmen didn't like to share secrets. "I know you have no reason to do this for me, but I'm going to ask you anyway. I have more than a million in a safe at my house back home. I want to make that into two hundred million. I want to go into business with you. I know my money doesn't sound like much to you, but it's all I got, and I worked just as hard as the next man to get it."

"Whoa, Malek, slow down," Gary said, holding

his hands up as if to halt Malek's words. "I'm not into the illegal thing. I don't want to jeopardize myself."

"I know. And I wouldn't even put you in that kind of position. My trip to these islands is kind of like a celebration of my retirement from the game. I'm not into that anymore. I just have this money sitting around, but it's not enough. I need stupid money. Any advice you can give me, I'd appreciate."

"Stupid money comes from stupid people. What you need, Malek, is legitimate and long money. If you're serious about staying out of the streets, then I'm willing to take a chance on you."

Malek clapped loudly and stood up.

"Don't get too excited too soon," Gary told him. "It's a process involved here, Malek." Gary stood up with him. "Until I clean all of that drug money you have, you have to stay out of the spotlight. No large purchases, no more expensive trips, nothing. Even the things you've already bought may be in jeopardy."

"The only big purchases we've made is the house and our two whips, both six Series Benzes," Malek explained. "Nothing too big." He shrugged his shoulders as if the average Joe Blow could make those types of purchases.

Gary couldn't help but laugh at his new friend's nonchalant attitude. "Those are huge purchases, Malek. But don't worry. I'll draw up some paperwork to legitimize those purchases."

He walked over to the liquor cabinet and poured them both a glass of cognac.

"Don't worry about it, Malek. I'll take care of it for you and, more importantly, teach you how to take care of it yourself." He handed Malek a glass then sat down in one of his twelve plush theater chairs.

Malek took a seat next to Gary. "Yo, G, you really don't know how much I appreciate you doing this for me."

"No need to thank me. You seem like a man who has put in enough work in his own right to really be able to enjoy life. Besides, your inquiry only confirms what I knew from the moment I ran into you and your lady over at the pier."

"Oh yeah?" Malek asked, curious about just how Gary had perceived him. "And what is that?"

"That you are someone who, like myself, stays hungry to achieve more in life. That you are satisfied with nothing, and therefore strive for everything. It's that same thing that got me to where I am today." Gary looked at Malek. "And I was right."

"You certainly were." Malek smiled. This time he was the first to raise his glass for a toast. "To a new partnership."

"And a new friendship," Gary added.

The next day, Malek accompanied Gary to his office to set up accounts in the islands and to

sign paperwork to legitimize the purchase of his cars and home.

"The accounts are through the Turks and Caicos Banks of the Caribbean. These accounts are set up so that only you and I can access them," Gary explained. "I cannot access them without you, and vice versa. I have made a deposit already with my own money to match what you said you have saved up. This partnership is contingent on a fifty-fifty split, so our initial investment is equal."

Gary nodded toward the statements Malek was looking over. "You can see proof of my deposit from the statement you have right there in your hands."

Malek looked over the statement and clearly saw the existing balance. "So how do I get my money to you?"

"When you arrive back to the States, you can call a friend of mine. Her name is Ashley Wagner, an accountant in Detroit. She can wire your money to the secure account I have set up," Gary explained. "I've already called her and explained everything to her, so she will be expecting you."

"Cool," Malek said with a nod, his blank facial expression masking his disbelief.

"Something wrong?" Gary asked, eyeballing the papers. "Did you find some type of discrepancy?"

Malek paused for a minute before he spoke. "No, it's not that." He paused once more.

"Then tell me. What is it?"

Malek took a deep breath then looked up at Gary. "It all makes sense, but at the same time, it doesn't. I mean, where I'm from, no way would cats share the wealth. The minute a nigga find out another nigga is seeking his wealth and riches, the last thing he does is bring him on board, because the first thing he does is arrange for his elimination from the game completely."

Gary put his hand on Malek's shoulder. "My friend, that's the difference between me and the men where you come from. I know that when I call myself helping someone out, in actuality, they are helping me out. We have each put ourselves in a position where one has no more to gain than the other, nor does one have any more to lose than the other. If for some reason our investments fail, then we both lose our money. You get me?"

"Yeah, but still, why me, some dude you just met and don't know from Adam? I mean, inviting me into your home was enough. Now you're inviting me into your finances."

"So you're a skeptic, huh?"

"No, it's not that. I'm just keeping it real. Back home, you have to prove yourself to get put on. I've done nothing, so I guess I'm just having a hard time understanding why you'd put me on."

"Like I told you, when I met you, I just knew there was something about you. You reminded me a lot of myself. My mother always said you know after one conversation whether you can

really trust someone. Well, I knew I could trust you, Malek. Now all you have to do is trust me." Gary held out his hand.

Malek looked down at it, smiled, and then shook it.

"So, as I was saying, I am coming back to the States at the end of the month, and when I arrive, we will choose some investments to get you started in. We will invest aggressively because we want to make as much money as we can while we're young. I invested in Starbucks before it became such a huge brand, and now I'm sitting on piles of money, so we will look for companies that have future earning potential.

"I know you've said that the money is your savings, so if you reach a point where you'll need to withdraw money from the account, just contact Ashley. She'll be your personal banker, and will set up the transaction for you without the IRS getting wind of it. It also puts your home and cars in the name of a dummy corporation so that the IRS won't inquire about the attainment of your home."

"Sounds easy enough," Malek said, papers still in hand. "Let's make it happen."

"Good." Gary pointed to the paperwork. "All I need you to do is sign here and here." He pulled out a pen from his shirt pocket and handed it to Malek.

Malek exhaled then signed. "Thanks, man. You don't know how much weight this has lifted off my shoulders. I don't have to worry about

having dirty money lying around for the government to take, or worry about someone trying to rob me."

"No problem. Just make sure you stay off the corner. Don't make me regret doing business with you."

"Never, fam," Malek responded.

"All right then, my friend, let's go enjoy your last night in the Caribbean."

Halleigh had been asleep for about two hours, but Malek just lay in the bed. He couldn't seem to get any sleep. He looked over at Halleigh and admired her beauty. It was true, what he had heard about the glow of a pregnant woman, because Halleigh looked even more beautiful. Pregnancy truly was becoming to her.

The couple had partied on the island all night, and Malek was exhausted, but his mind was racing. The endless possibilities of becoming successful the legit way had him excited. Players in the game always talked about giving up the street life and going legit, although few ever really could overpower the allure of the game. Looking at the success of his new friend, Malek knew his chances were much better than most.

Malek looked around the guest room. *This is just what I need,* he thought. *I can really establish a good future for my child and Halleigh.* Coming on this vacation and running into Gary had to be

fate, as everything was falling right in line with his and Halleigh's plan to leave the hood life for the good life.

Feeling a little bit parched, Malek got up slowly, making sure he didn't wake Halleigh, who was sleeping so comfortably. He headed downstairs. As he stood in the kitchen getting a drink, he heard voices in the living room. He put the glass down and headed toward the voices.

Malek crept into the living room, and what he saw blew his mind. A totally naked woman—for some reason, he thought she was Brazilian—was performing oral sex on Marie while they lay on a bearskin rug.

Marie moaned. She was resting on her elbows, her head thrown back and her legs opened wide. Gary was in back of the Brazilian-looking woman, sexing her while she partook of what Marie had to offer.

Malek was in the doorway, and they didn't see him. He wanted to leave and not watch, but his eyes couldn't come off the erotic escapade.

They all seemed to be on the same page as they sexed each other in perfect harmony. He watched as the perfect, perky breasts of the Brazilian woman swung against Marie's inner thighs every time Gary gave her a thrust. He then looked at Marie, who now lay flat on her back, massaging her own breasts while getting oral pleasure.

Malek was in complete shock. He had never

seen anything so beautiful. It wasn't like some nasty porno tape. It all seemed so well rehearsed and orchestrated. It was as if he was in a dream state as he watched.

Marie sat up and turned around so that the woman could taste her from behind. With her back arched like a cat, she looked under her, in order to witness the woman's tongue teasing her clit. That's when she got a glimpse of someone in her peripheral view. She quickly looked toward the entrance and saw Malek standing there. She was startled by his presence, but she didn't let the others know. She just continued to grind her body against the other woman's face while looking seductively into Malek's eyes. It seemed as though Malek's voyeurism was the icing on Marie's cake, as it turned her on even more.

Malek, though intrigued at first, was now totally uncomfortable, knowing that Marie was watching him watching them. He felt like a pervert. He tensed up and started to back away, but that's when Marie stood up and walked away from the woman, who was moaning and groaning in ecstasy from the treatment Gary was delivering to her.

Marie made her way over to Malek. Everything in him told him to continue backing away, but he was hypnotized by the vision before him. He looked at the long, slender body and admired the tantalizing view.

Marie, without saying a word, grabbed Malek's

hand and guided him into the party. When Gary and the woman saw that they had a new participant, they didn't lose a step.

Marie dropped down on all fours and grabbed Malek's already rock-hard tool from the slit in his boxer shorts. Before he could refuse her offer, she'd taken him into her mouth. Malek quickly looked over his shoulder, making sure Halleigh wasn't coming, then turned his attention back to Marie and watched her go to work on him.

"Ohh, uhh, ohh," the Brazilian woman and Gary moaned as they climaxed together.

Before Malek knew it, the Brazilian woman left her position on all fours in front of Gary and joined in with Marie on the blowjob.

"Mmm," Marie moaned. The women were taking turns licking Malek and then each other's tongues.

"Oh shit!" Malek had never been more turned on in his life. He rotated his hips to the rhythm of the women's tongues as they took turns sucking harder and fondling him. He knew it was only a matter of time before he exploded in their mouths.

It wasn't long before Malek saw Halleigh's face. Not in the flesh, but in his mind. Suddenly a wave of guilt overtook him, and he pulled away from the two women, exiting the room the same way he had come. His conscience wouldn't let him indulge any further. There was only one woman he ever wanted to take him to such a

level of ecstasy, and that was Halleigh, the mother of his soon-to-be-born child.

Malek ran back up the stairs and got in bed with Halleigh, this time waking her.

"You're still up, baby?" Halleigh asked as she cuddled under his arm. She could feel his heart beating rapidly. "Are you okay?"

"Yeah, I'm fine. Go back to sleep," Malek said as he wrapped his arms around her. He couldn't believe what he'd just witnessed. Even more so, he couldn't believe what he'd just done. Although he felt guilt, he had to admit it was exciting. Gary was living the high life, and Malek definitely wanted a piece of it. All of it!

Chapter Ten

Halleigh and Malek hated to say good-bye to Marie and Gary. They had grown close in a short amount of time, but it was time for them to get back to the real world. Flint awaited them. And although it pained them to just think about landing on the soil that would take them back to that town, they felt better knowing they wouldn't be there for long. They had their new home to look forward to.

The couple wished they could pull strings like Gary had and just have someone go to their place, pack up all of their things, and deliver it to their new domain. But that wasn't realistic. Besides, Malek had a couple of loose ends he needed to mend. So, Halleigh and Malek packed up all their things and prepared to say farewell to their new friends.

Marie hugged Halleigh tightly and said, "Oh, take care of yourself, sweetheart." She rubbed

Halleigh's stomach. "And take care of that baby too."

"I will," Halleigh assured her, returning the hug. "I had so much fun. You take care too," she replied. "Hopefully, once Malek and I get settled and situated after the baby is born, we can return."

"That would be great. Perhaps make it an annual thing."

"Sounds good to me," Malek said as he came down the steps with luggage in hand. "That's if Gary here doesn't mind." He looked at Gary, who was standing next to Marie.

"Of course I don't mind . . . partner." Gary winked and shook Malek's hand. "Farewell, my friend. We'll be in touch."

"Yes, we will." Malek nodded.

Gary and Malek shook hands. Their good-bye was less emotional than that of the women. For one, they were men, and two, they knew they would be seeing each other again soon.

"I've arranged a car for you. It's waiting out front," Gary told the couple. He and Marie walked them out to the car and bid them one last farewell as the car pulled off.

Halleigh wasn't looking forward to the long airplane ride. It was much more exciting heading toward the destination than returning from it. Besides that, she was beat and needed the comfort of a bed. She'd told herself she would sleep during the entire flight. That way, maybe it wouldn't seem so long; but her discomfort

wouldn't allow her to doze off. To make the time go by, she decided to strike up a conversation with Malek. Finding a subject matter wasn't difficult, since Gary had said something that piqued her curiosity.

"What did Gary mean when he referred to you as his partner?" Halleigh said to Malek just as he was about to finally doze off.

"Huh?"

"Gary called you *partner* and then winked," Halleigh told him. "He even said that he'd be in touch, like you have some business to take care of."

Just the thought of the business that he and Gary had to take care of put a smile on Malek's face. "I was going to wait to tell you, you know, once the money got flipped and everything."

Before Malek could say another word, Halleigh snapped. "I knew it. I didn't want to ask because I really didn't want to know. But I knew Gary was someone involved in the drug business. And now he's pulling you back in." Halleigh slammed her fist against her knee. "And I have no one to blame but myself, insisting we stay there and—"

"Halleigh." Malek chuckled, cutting her off.

"Oh, you think it's funny, Malek? You think it's funny that you broke a promise?" Halleigh's eyes began to water.

"Baby, listen," Malek said in a serious tone. "You've got it all wrong. Gary doesn't deal in the drug trade. He earned everything he has the le-

gitimate way. He's into stocks, investments, and all that good stuff, and—get this—he's going to put me on. He's gonna teach me the tricks of the trade so that I can be in his shoes someday, and hopefully soon."

Halleigh paused for a minute, staring into Malek's eyes. "You serious?" she asked, wiping her eyes dry.

"As a heart attack, baby." Malek ran his hand down Halleigh's hair. "I told you that you could trust me, and that I'd always take care of you. Believe that, baby. It's happening. It's really happening."

Halleigh couldn't do anything but smile and picture their new life together as he explained to her the business deal he'd struck with Gary. Although she didn't quite understand all of the specifics, she was happy to hear it because now she knew for sure that Malek wasn't going back to the streets. No longer would she doubt her man's intentions. She could honestly say that for the first time, for real this time, she felt one hundred percent secure in her life and her future with Malek.

"I'm so proud of you, baby," she said.

"To tell you the truth, so am I . . . so am I."

Malek and Halleigh entered their home, and although it was nothing like Gary's, it was theirs and they'd missed it. The two never thought they'd see the day where they would miss anything about Flint, but they did.

Malek and Halleigh shed all of their clothing. They were too tired to even shower before they passed out in their king-sized bed. The two slept through the night and well into the morning before they were interrupted by the buzzing of the alarm clock on Malek's cell phone.

"Shut it off," Halleigh moaned as she put her pillow over her head and returned to sleep.

Malek reluctantly got up and turned off the alarm. He didn't want to wake up yet, but he had business to handle that couldn't wait. He had to put the nail in the coffin that would seal his and Gary's deal.

Malek got showered and dressed. Then he packaged all of his money from his safe into two briefcases. He kissed a sleeping Halleigh on the head before whispering, "I'll be back."

Halleigh didn't respond, but he knew she'd heard him, by the soft moan she released and the shift in her position.

Malek got into his car and headed for Detroit to meet with Gary's accountant, who would be his accountant, too, once he hit her with his million and change. As he drove, even though he hadn't profited a dime yet, for some reason he felt like he'd already accomplished something. He was going legit. He knew Jamaica Joe would have been proud.

"Mama," Malek said as he drove, "I know you'd be proud of me too." He smiled as his GPS system guided him directly to his destination.

Malek pulled into the parking lot of the ac-

countant's building. It was a glass office building that sat in the middle of downtown. He picked up his cell phone and dialed Gary's number, wanting to make sure everything was still all good.

"Malek, how's it going?" Gary answered. "I'm glad to see you made it home safely."

"Yeah, thanks. I just wanted to let you know that I'm about to meet with your girl Ashley now. I'm outside of her office. Is everything still good?"

"It's all good, my friend. And so is Ashley. She's the best in the business. She'll take care of you. I've already faxed her all of the documents," Gary said. "She has everything she needs." Gary cleared his throat. "That is, with one exception, of course."

"Not to worry." Malek looked at the briefcases that rested on the passenger's seat. "I got it all here with me."

"Good."

"So, let me head on in here, and I'll talk to you later, fam. I don't want to be late," Malek stated, knowing that tardiness in the professional sector was frowned upon. Hell, even in the streets when a nigga was supposed to meet up with him at a certain time and didn't come through it was frowned upon. Malek just figured, when it came to money, shit always needed to be on time.

Malek closed his cell phone and proceeded into the building. When he found her office, he

entered. The receptionist wasn't at her desk, so he stood and waited nervously. He didn't know why his nerves were getting the better of him. Perhaps he just felt that it was all too good to be true.

He didn't have to wait too long before an older white woman appeared from the closed door behind the desk.

"I'm sorry to have you waiting. My receptionist is at lunch. You must be Malek," she greeted with an extended hand. "I hope you weren't waiting too long."

"Actually, I just got here," Malek told her, shaking her hand. "I'm Malek, and it's nice to meet you, Ms. Wagner." He held up the two briefcases. "I have the money to deposit into my account."

"Right this way," she said as she led Malek to her office, back through the doorway she'd just come through.

The white walls and floor-to-ceiling windows gave the room a bright look. Malek sat in the chair across from her glass desk, on which a laptop sat, and she took her place behind it.

"How much did you want to deposit?" she asked.

"It's a million and some change," he answered. He opened each briefcase and revealed the money to her.

She closed the briefcases without even counting the money and put them underneath her desk.

"Now, if you need to access these accounts or need assistance adding up interest or dividends, just call me. You have my card. We can meet once a month to make sure everything is going smoothly, if that works for you."

"That's fine," he answered.

She removed some papers from her desk and handed them to Malek. "On the last page, please fill in the amount of money you are depositing, and then sign by the X."

Malek quickly filled in the information and put his signature on the paper. He was too busy thinking about how rich we was going to be to even read all the fine print on the page. He handed them back to Ms. Wagner.

"Thank you." She smiled. "Now, what day works best for you next month, so we can meet to talk about how much your investment has earned?"

"The first is good," he responded. "Pretty easy to remember."

"The first it is then, Mr. Johnson." She scribbled on her calendar. "How about one o'clock?"

"One o'clock is good."

Ms. Wagner stood, signaling that their meeting was over.

"Is that it?" Malek asked.

"That's it," she replied. "For now anyway."

The transaction was easier than Malek thought it would be. He was sure there'd be more paperwork for him to sign, but obviously Gary had taken care of absolutely everything. This made

Malek feel even more confident about his partnership with Gary, a man, like himself, who handled his business.

Malek shook her hand once more and left the office feeling like a new man. He was now a businessman and was stepping into the majors.

Chapter Eleven

Malek drove down I-75 on his way to his appointment with Ms. Wagner. It had been a month since he had turned over his money to the accountant to get cleaned. It was now the first of the month, which meant it was time to go check up on his investments. He was excited to see what dividends he'd made on his money. It had only been a short time, but he had learned that in the world of high finance, so much could transpire in a month. During one of his and Gary's discussion back at the island, Gary had hit him up on a time when he tripled his money in only one week. Malek would be more than satisfied to simply double his money.

Malek and Gary had been touching base on the telephone all month. They had arranged to meet up in Miami on the upcoming weekend to talk face to face. Hopefully, after his visit with Ms. Wagner, they'd be celebrating as well.

Malek finally reached his destination. He pulled into the parking lot and stepped out of the car feeling like a million bucks. Over the past month, just the mere thought of going legit had him feeling ahead of the game and prepared for the future. He'd managed to stay free and clear from the game, with the exception of the couple of times Mitch had hit him up with a few questions regarding contacts and whatnot.

As he walked up to the office, he noticed something strange. It looked like there was no light shining through the vertical blinds covering the office window. From a distance, the place looked closed.

The closer Malek got, the quicker he picked up his pace, with a sick feeling growing in the pit of his stomach. Upon arriving at the double doors to Ms. Wagner's office, his concern grew worse. He turned the knob and pulled on the door. It didn't budge. It was locked.

Malek nervously looked down at his watch. "One o'clock," he said out loud. He was exactly on time. He tried the door again, hoping that maybe it had just gotten jammed or something and would open this time. Unfortunately, that wasn't the case.

Looking down at his watch yet again, Malek tried to ignore his nerves, telling himself that perhaps Ms. Wagner had just gone to lunch or something and hadn't made it back. As his blood pressure rose, so did his suspicions. As

much as he didn't want to admit it, he was starting to understand the real deal.

Hesitantly, he exited the building and walked over to the window. He pressed his hands to block off the sun's glare, and stared into the room where he and Ms. Wagner had done business—the room where he had handed over pretty much every dime he had.

With a clear view of the office, he quickly discovered that what just one month ago had looked like a well put-together accounting office was now a vacant suite. "No fucking way!" He went back inside the building and tried the office door again. "Fuck!" Malek spat as the thoughts he'd tried to suppress began to rise.

Malek's heart dropped when he looked down and saw a shiny piece of paper with a piece of tape on it. He picked it up and turned it over, only to discover that it was a sign that read: OFFICE SPACE AVAILABLE FOR RENT. It must have fallen off the door.

"Son of a bitch!" Malek yelled as he stormed away from the building.

As he made his way back to the car, he called the number he'd reached Ms. Wagner on before. He heard a recorded voice saying that the number was disconnected.

Malek began to panic. He looked down at the phone to make sure he had dialed the correct number. Although it appeared he had, he still punched in the numbers again. He got the same response from the automated operator.

"Fuck!" Malek yelled as he gripped the phone tightly and pushed the end button. It took everything he had not to throw the phone across the parking lot and through the vacant office window. Instead, he surfed through his phonebook contacts and retrieved Gary's number. Malek couldn't wait to tell Gary about the sheisty accountant. He knew Gary would be just as pissed. After all, he had deposited more than a million dollars with her as well.

As Malek waited for the call to go through, he tried to convince himself that everything was just a misunderstanding. "That bitch better had moved her office or something," he said to himself as he waited for Gary to pick up the ringing phone. But after a few seconds, an operator's voice notified Malek that Gary's number was no longer in service.

This couldn't be right. Malek had just spoken with Gary less than five minutes ago.

This time, Malek pulled up his calling log on his cell phone. Gary was the last person he'd called, so he simply redialed the number he'd just spoken to him on. When he heard the operator repeat her same spiel, the phone almost slipped from his hand.

"I promise to God, Ashton Kutcher's ass better pop out from somewhere and tell me I'm being punked or else—" Malek gritted his teeth.

Malek's hands began to sweat, and his heart was beating a thousand times per minute. He couldn't believe he had been swindled. *This*

can't be happening. He scrolled through his phone and found Gary's office number. When he got the same recorded response, he knew for sure he'd been set up.

Malek jumped into his car, and out of frustration, pulled out his gun. He then got back out of the car, walked back toward the office, and emptied his entire clip through the office window. He stormed back to his car determined to be on the first thing smoking back to the island. He was about to go straight to Gary and see what was going on.

Malek was racking his brain on the whole plane ride back to the islands. He didn't want to worry Halleigh, so he didn't tell her about the mishap. He'd simply told her that he needed to meet with Gary face to face to handle some business. He didn't want to stress her out until he found out for sure what was going on. It was probably nothing but a misunderstanding—at least, that's what he kept trying to tell himself. But it had been two days since he'd tried to contact both the accountant and Gary, and he hadn't heard from either one of them. Up until that point, he and Gary had pretty much talked on a regular basis.

Even if it turned out that Gary was on the up-and-up and had nothing to do with the accountant going MIA, Malek planned on holding him accountable, since Gary had hooked the whole

thing up. He was going to get his money back, one way or the other. And if Gary was behind this whole scam from the beginning, Malek had made up his mind that Gary would have to pay him back or else pay with his life.

His intentions were to pay Gary a surprise visit. He knew Gary would never expect him to pop up on him so quick, but he was about to bring the heat right to his front door.

Just hours later, Malek was at Gary's house. He banged on the front door after ringing the doorbell repeatedly and getting no answer. After a while, someone finally unlocked the door. Malek breathed a sigh of relief, but was somewhat puzzled by the person who stood on the other side of the door.

"Hello, sir. Are you my one o'clock appointment?" the professionally dressed woman with clipboard in hand asked as she extended her hand for a shake.

"I'm looking for Gary Williams," he said as he frowned in confusion.

"Oh, I'm sorry. Gary Williams only rented this villa out for the month. This is the property of Prestige Rentals, sir," she said confidently.

Malek wasn't trying to hear anything she had to say. For all he knew, she was just someone Gary told to get rid of him while he relaxed in another room.

Before the woman could say another word, Malek brushed past her and entered the house. "Gary! Gary!" He stormed around the house fu-

riously. "Where the fuck are you?" he yelled as he searched the placed. He noticed that the few pictures of Gary and Marie that he'd seen around the house before were now gone. That's when he finally admitted to himself that his suspicions were true—He had been got.

"Sir! Sir, excuse me," the woman said as she struggled to keep up with Malek's pace. "I'm not sure what's going on, but like I said, Mr. Williams is not here. This is not his residence. Never was. It's a timeshare rental. Now, if you're interested in renting this property, then by all means we can talk business, but if you are here for any other reason, then I'm going to have to ask you to excuse yourself."

Malek just stood there breathing hard, casting an evil glare on the woman. He hadn't meant to be intimidating to her, but he couldn't help himself. This wasn't like one of his contacts shorting him on some dope, or one of his corner boys shorting him on some change. This was more than a million dollars at stake. This was his life. This was his future. Not just his future, but the future of Halleigh and his unborn child.

"I'm sorry, sir," the woman said, trying her best not to show any fear, although her trembling hands were a dead giveaway. "You have to leave, or I am going to be forced to call the cops," the real estate agent said.

"Fuck the cops!" Malek yelled just before he stormed out the door. With no other leads on how to contact Gary, Malek decided all he could

do was go home. But then he remembered the office Gary had given him a tour of. Only thing was, he couldn't remember the name of the facility, nor where it was located. He didn't know what to do next, but he knew he couldn't give up, not just yet.

Malek sat on the plane on his way home, still trying to understand the fact that he had just lost everything he'd worked for. He'd hired a driver to escort him around, looking for the facility which Gary claimed housed his company. He was sure that they had covered every inch of the island, but it was to no avail. Malek was, once again, disappointed by his lack of results. At this point, though, he knew that even if he had found the building, it would most likely be vacated, just like the bogus accountant's office.

Malek felt like he'd lost his mind, like Michael Douglas in the movie *The Game.* He kept replaying the scenes in his head, starting from the moment Gary showed up to save the day at the pier. He wondered how he missed seeing the snake in the grass. While he was worrying about why Gary would trust him enough to go into business with him, he should have been asking himself why he should trust that fool. How could he have been so stupid to get caught up in the entire fantasy of the good life?

Everything had seemed so real, like destiny was unfolding and Gary was a part of it. In those

few days Malek spent with the millionaire, he hadn't detected anything shady. Nor did he sense anything strange during any of their phone conversations. Unfortunately, Malek had to blame his lack of experience in the "real world." Now he was paying for it.

Had it just been his future at stake, Malek would have simply chalked it up as a loss and kept moving, but that wasn't the case. He buried his face in his hands as he wondered how he would explain to Halleigh that he had been swindled, and that they now only had $10,000 to their names. He was grateful that he had kept even that little somethin'-somethin' to tide them over until his money made a profit. He had been tempted to put all of it in the hands of that accountant, and then he and Halleigh would have been penniless now.

How could I not see this shit? Malek threw his head back against the coach seat. Just a month ago he'd been enjoying the good life of first class; now he was back in coach. And just when he thought there was no place left to go but up, everything was going right back down. In the past, he had always managed to come out on top no matter what. Now, he just couldn't imagine how he'd be able to pull that off one more time.

Chapter Twelve

As the moonlight shone into the room, Malek stood near the window and stared at Halleigh, who slept peacefully in their bed. He couldn't manage to get any sleep, knowing he had no money to take care of her and their unborn seed. It had been a couple of days since he returned from the islands, and every time he thought about telling Halleigh that he was swindled out of their life savings, he couldn't go through with it.

A part of him wanted to take the ten grand he had left and go flip it on the streets to avoid ever having to tell her. The last thing he wanted to witness was the look of disappointment on her face when she found out they were broke. He knew without a doubt he could once again reach millionaire status by getting back in the game. Although he had already vowed to leave the

streets of Flint alone, things had changed. That promise was made before he found himself back at square one.

He slowly paced the room, trying to think of a way to make things right, but all of his ideas led back to the hustling. He didn't want to break his promise to Halleigh, but his back was up against the wall. His options were slim to none.

He clenched his jaws as he walked over to the nightstand and picked up his phone. He didn't want to do what he was about to do, but the way he saw it, he was between a rock and a hard place. Either way it went, he'd be letting Halleigh down. If there was a slim chance that he could grind without Halleigh ever finding out, he was more than willing to take that chance.

Slipping out of the bedroom with phone in hand, Malek scrolled through the contacts and dialed a number he never thought in a million years he'd be dialing. "Just a couple of flips and I'm out," he whispered to himself as he walked into the living room so his conversation wouldn't wake Halleigh.

Malek stood in front of the window as he listened to the ringing on the other end. Like Jay-Z, it was time for him to make one more brief appearance in the game. Yeah, he was about to dive back into the game, but with a purpose this time.

* * *

Mitch drove down I-75 on his way back from meeting Fredro, his coke connect. It was nearly two in the morning, and the highway was clear and calm, just the way he liked it. He was able to cruise free and clear while listening to his stereo pump out his famous tunes. This always made him feel as though he was on top of the world— as did the fact that he had just negotiated a deal to bring a hundred kilos of coke back to Flint. It was the biggest order Fredro had filled since he had been supplying the city of Flint. Mitch couldn't believe how major he had become, and how quickly.

Mitch was preparing to take over the North and South sides of the city with an iron fist, and nothing or no one could stop him. He envisioned being the most notorious player Flint would ever know. Unlike Malek, it didn't matter how much money he banked; he wasn't giving up life on the streets. Even in corporate America, Mitch couldn't think of one millionaire who didn't want another million. And, by any means necessary, he was going to make sure the money continued to flow.

Mitch didn't have a beef with Sweets like Malek did, and he was prepared to put the war aside to make money. *Violence only begets more violence, which means police.* Mitch thought about how much money he was about to get as he switched lanes.

Since Sweets had agreed to cop coke from

him, Mitch could, and did, set his prices as high as he wanted in the streets, seeing that his main competition, the person who had kept him from being "the man" in the streets, was out of the game anyway. A smile spread across Mitch's face. Malek was no longer a threat to him.

Just as quickly as the smile had appeared, it was gone, thanks to thoughts of Keesha's antagonizing words resurfacing and echoing through his mind. He thought about all that time he'd worked under Malek, and about the number of people who must have seen him the same way Keesha did—just a flunky sidekick to Malek. Even though Malek was now out of the game and cats in the streets were dealing with Mitch, a trace of jealousy was still evident in his heart.

Mitch clenched his jaws just as his cell phone vibrated in his pocket. Keeping his eyes on the road and erasing thoughts of his predecessor, he answered the phone.

"Mitch, what's good?" the caller asked.

Mitch almost went left of center at the sound of the caller's voice. He wanted to kick himself for thinking him up. "What up?" he responded, instantly getting aggravated by the sound of Malek's voice.

"Shit all bad right now. I got caught up in some bullshit, and I need back in."

A huge lump formed in Mitch's throat. "What you mean, you need back in?"

Mitch hoped Malek didn't mean what he

thought he meant, but Malek quickly confirmed his biggest fear.

"I need back in the game. I need to go meet with Fredro and get hit with something," Malek said, telling him more than asking.

Mitch didn't even have to think twice about his response. The game wasn't big enough for both him and Malek. "I don't think that's going to happen, homeboy," he said, hate in his voice.

"What? What you mean?" Malek asked, not believing what he was hearing.

"You heard me, nigga. It ain't happening."

Malek couldn't fully understand the sudden change in Mitch. The last they talked, everything was all good, so he couldn't imagine what had changed between then and now. "Mitch, what's the problem, fam?"

Mitch started, "I'm not the one with the problem! You—"

Malek cut him off, screaming through the phone, "Who the fuck is you talking to, nigga?" Had Mitch forgotten just that quickly who put him on? Just in case he did, Malek felt the urge to remind him. "I put you in the position you are in right now. You sound like a damn fool, telling me what I can and can't do. What's got into you, fam?"

"I'm boss now. If you want in, you can work one of the blocks in the Fifth Ward."

"Work a block? I move bricks. I hit niggas that work on blocks. I'm not a worker, or did you for-

get? I don't know what has gotten into you, but all that shit gon' change when I get in Flint. Don't let the money go to your head, fam, for real."

"Fuck you! Come see me then, nigga. You know where I'm at, son," Mitch said menacingly, totally losing his cool.

"I see it's too late. Shit done already went to your head. I guess now your ass think you the king of Flint now, huh? Well, we'll see if you singing that tune later, homeboy!" Malek yelled then hung up.

Mitch smiled as he flipped down his phone, his ego fed, knowing he had just demeaned Malek. Hell, Malek should have been grateful that he'd even offered to put him on in any kind of way. When he turned over the reigns, it was a done deal. Mitch wasn't about to let Malek climb back up on his white horse and come riding back to Flint like some knight in shining armor. He had his chance at the top and had given it all up. Now, if he wanted back in, he had to start at the bottom.

Mitch couldn't control his excitement. For the first time, Malek would know what it felt like to play second fiddle.

Malek was furious as he flipped his phone down, not believing what he had just heard. "I put him on. He got the nerve to think he's

going to stop me from getting back in. I am Flint!" Malek said, talking to himself.

As Malek paced back and forth in anger, he saw a figure in his peripheral view. It was Halleigh in her nightgown, looking as beautiful as ever, as she yawned and stretched her arms out.

"Why are you still up, baby?" she asked, seeing the concerned looked on Malek's face.

"Just thinking," Malek said, still trying to figure out how to tell her that he'd just lost everything they had.

Halleigh walked over to Malek and began to rub his shoulders. "Want to talk about it?"

Malek was burning on the inside, not only because of his situation, but because of the way Mitch had showed total disloyalty. Back to back, he had been completely wrong about the character of the people he'd decided to do business with.

"No, I'm good," Malek answered Halleigh. "I'll handle it. Just go back to sleep, baby."

Malek headed toward the bedroom, and Halleigh followed behind him. She climbed back into bed, thinking that's where Malek was headed. Instead, he walked over to his dresser, opened drawers, and began slipping on some clothes.

"Where are you going?"

"I'ma take a ride just to clear my head, okay?"

Halleigh sat up in the bed, a worried expres-

sion on her face. "You sure everything is all right, Malek?"

Malek turned and looked into the eyes of the woman he'd die for. As much as he wanted to just crawl up in the bed next to her and tell her everything, he couldn't. He couldn't admit that he'd let her down.

"Everything is going to be all right, I promise." Malek nodded his head up and down, all the while putting a plan together in his head to try to make things all right.

Mitch watched his sweat drip onto the small of Keesha's back as he grinded her deeply and slowly. She had been waiting for him to return from seeing Fredro so they could live out their planned sexual escapade, and that's exactly what they were doing. Mitch watched as his pelvic area hit Keesha's behind, and a small wave went through her fat ass cheeks. He gripped her love handles as he dug her out, enjoying every minute of it.

"Mitch! Ooh, baby! That's the spot right there," she said as she gripped the bed sheets tightly and bit down on her bottom lip so hard that for a minute there, she thought she'd drawn blood. He was thrusting in and out of her so hard that it hurt so good.

"Who's the boss?" Mitch smacked Keesha's ass.

"You are," she moaned.

"Who?" He smacked her again.

"You are."

"I'm what? Say that shit! Say it!"

"You're the boss!" Keesha exclaimed as she climaxed.

Mitch pumped harder and harder as Keesha declared him the boss. That alone was turning him on more than the actual sex. He smiled as he thought about being the head nigga in charge. He had just put Malek in his place and he felt damn good about it. He pumped faster and harder as he thought about the demeaning comments Keesha had been making about him being under Malek, as if he wasn't boss.

Mitch was so busy trying to blow Keesha's back out, he never heard Malek creeping up behind him. The cold steel from the gun startled him as Malek pressed it to the back of his head.

"Surprise, mu'fucka!" Malek said from behind Mitch.

"Aghhh!" Keesha screamed as she turned around and scooted to the corner of the bed. She watched Mitch on his knees at gunpoint.

"Shut the fuck up!" Malek said to Keesha through clenched teeth, giving her a stare colder than the winter in January.

Keesha immediately stopped her yelling, knowing what was best for her.

Malek turned his attention back to Mitch. "Nigga, I can get to you anytime I want. Remem-

ber who the fuck I am. I'm cut from the cloth of Jamaica Joe. Remember that!" Malek pulled back the hammer on his gun.

Mitch was frozen in fear, and it was written all over his face. He'd just forced Keesha to declare that he was boss. Now he sat in front of her looking like a bitch-ass nigga.

"Turn around and look at me in my eyes." Malek nudged Mitch in the head with his gun.

Mitch slowly turned around with his hands in the air and then looked in the eyes of the man he'd just betrayed.

"I can get to you anyplace, anytime. You can't push me out the game. I am Flint!" Malek said, getting louder with each word. He pointed the gun at Keesha and watched as she squirmed and her face became flush.

He released a small chuckle and then exited the room. He could have very well taken Mitch out right then and there, but that wasn't his intention. He was playing mental chess with Mitch, and just wanted to show him who was still boss.

Mitch's heart was beating double-time as he collapsed on the bed. It felt as if it would jump out of his chest. Not only was his heart racing, but his blood was boiling too. Mitch was furious. He hated that Malek just had his life in his hands and played with him like a cat did its prey.

Now it's war.

Mitch was breathing heavily. He heard the sound of his front door slam shut. Malek might have just slammed the door closed behind him, but he'd just opened up a new chapter to a novel—one that was sure not to have such a happy ending.

Chapter Thirteen

Scratch sat with his old friend, Sharina, who was still pretty upset over the shooting at the rehab center. She had come back to Flint after getting sober, hoping that she could fix things with Halleigh. But that never happened, because the shots rang out before they had a chance to talk.

After Halleigh was whisked away in an ambulance, Sharina had searched every hospital until she found her daughter. She still wanted to clear the air and apologize for everything that had happened in the past. Scratch, who held a special place in his heart for both of them, was really hoping they could patch things up. He was almost as disappointed as Sharina when she came back and told him that she'd found Halleigh, who basically just told her to get the hell out of her life.

Scratch had grown close to Halleigh ever

since they met up on the streets. He felt a special connection to her because he remembered her mother from back in the day. He even started calling her Li'l Rina. First they were get-high partners when Halleigh was working for Manolo and using drugs to escape the pain. She finally cleaned herself up, but then stayed by Scratch's side and supported him while he was at the rehab center getting sober.

They had a special bond. He thought maybe if he went and talked to Halleigh, he could convince her to give her mother a second chance. Being newly sober himself, Scratch felt like even the worst addicts deserved a chance.

He looked for her, but no one in the streets had seen or heard from Halleigh since she got released from the hospital. It was as if she'd fallen off the face of the earth. Scratch felt obligated to stay close by Sharina's side. He was afraid that if she got too depressed about Halleigh, she might start getting high again. That's why he hated to tell her the bad news.

"I tried to find her, but no one has seen her. I put word out that I was looking to get in touch with her, though." Even if he did find her, Scratch couldn't help but wonder if Halleigh would even want to hear about her mother.

Scratch put his hand on Sharina's shoulder. "I'm sure she's gonna come and see you sooner or later," he said, giving her false hope out of the pity he felt for her.

Sharina didn't mind grasping at every little

bit of hope dealt to her either. "Yeah, I sure do hope so. I have so many things to ask for forgiveness for, ya know." Sharina sighed sadly. "I never was much of a mother to her, and I still have so much to say to my baby."

Scratch listened and nodded in complete understanding of Sharina's words. He, too, had some demons that he was battling. One in particular that he wanted to hide from Sharina was the fact that he was responsible for introducing her daughter to drugs. He felt so guilty, but knew that he would never tell Sharina. What good would it do to tell her? The whole thing ate him up every time he thought about it.

"Keep trying to find her, will you?" Sharina told Scratch, desperation in her eyes. Sharina then turned away in defeat. "Even though, if you do find her, she probably won't come racing to see me no-how." Sharina shook her head as her eyes watered.

"Don't talk like that. Li'l Rina will come around eventually. I'll make sure of it," Scratch assured her. Then he gave her a peck on the cheek and exited the room.

Scratch was going to find out where Halleigh was at, but he didn't know where to start. He'd looked under every rock in Flint to no avail. She had just simply vanished. But she had to be somewhere. For the sake of Sharina, he wasn't going to give up.

Scratch walked down the street headed to the homeless shelter, where he planned on trying to

get a place in line, so he could have a roof over his head for the night. He knew it was on a first-come, first-serve basis. They didn't hold a bed for nobody.

He walked with a pimp's swagger, and even though his bones were worn out, he still managed to have that same ol' stride he was once notorious for, before he allowed drugs to get the better of him. He hummed the sounds of an Isley Brothers tune as he walked past the same block where he used to score his dope. It was hard being a recovering addict, but he promised himself he would fly straight and get the monkey off his back for good.

Every time he got the urge to put the drug that once controlled his mind and body into his system, he quickly remembered how his inner demons took over when chasing the high. He would do any and everything just to score the drug. He learned firsthand that no matter what a dopefiend said he wouldn't do, when it all came down to it, he'd do it in a heartbeat. Scratch had been one of those fiends.

Ostracized by his entire family because of his addiction, in the end, he was left with nothing and nobody. His family and close friends turned their backs on him, locking their doors closed when they saw him walking down the street. The days of being invited to family Thanksgiving and Christmas dinners had become a thing of the past. Although it hurt Scratch, he couldn't even

be mad at his peoples. They had every reason to disown him.

Scratch would constantly scheme and swindle just to achieve his next high, even if it meant cheating and stealing from his own family. He remembered one time on Christmas, they were all having dinner at his mother's house, and his twelve-year-old niece had gotten a purse for Christmas with a hundred dollars in it. She wasn't aware that she couldn't just leave her purse lying around, even though it was only with family. No one explained to her that when one of the family members is a crackhead, the rules change.

In all honesty, Scratch hadn't set out to steal from his family that Christmas Day. As a matter of fact, he'd been clean for almost a week and was quite proud of himself; but when he walked into the bathroom and saw that purse just lying there next to the hand towels, he couldn't resist the temptation. He knew it was just a kid's purse and probably didn't have any money in it, but, out of habit, he had to see for himself.

He picked up the purse, unzipped it, and to his surprise, five pairs of eyes were staring up at him—all belonging to Andrew Jackson. Scratch counted out the five twenty-dollar bills. That's when the tug-of-war within himself began. He put the hundred dollars down in his pocket then headed to the bathroom door. Before he could even leave the room, he pulled the money back out of his pocket and stared at it. "I can't

do this," he told himself. He headed back over to the purse. "I don't need this," he reasoned as he placed the money back inside the purse. "I'm not even gonna get high no more."

Once again he walked away, but then that little voice spoke to him, calling him a fool for not holding on to at least some of the money . . . just in case he felt the urge to get high. On that note, Scratch took twenty dollars, leaving only eighty in his niece's purse.

"I could have taken it all. At least I left her most of it," he told himself, which allowed him to sleep that night. But by morning, the guilt had eaten him up to the point where only one thing could wash away the guilt—getting high.

Once the family discovered that there was a missing twenty-dollar bill, they didn't even have to think twice about how it had vanished. Stealing from a child was the ultimate low, as far as Scratch's family was concerned, and they let it be known to him by disowning him. Everyone cut him off, including his own mother.

Today, after all these years of getting high, Scratch was determined to never go that route again. He was ready to turn over a new leaf. He knew it could be done. It just wasn't going to be easy. And although the homeless shelter wasn't a place he wanted to call home forever, it was a start. He'd have to prove himself to the world all over again that he could be trusted and that he wanted to change.

Maybe Scratch will even get a job 'round these parts.

I still got swagger, he thought as he touched the tip of his brim and walked past the dope house he used to cop at, which Mitch now ran.

Malek sat back and watched as the crackheads and dopefiends went in and out of one of his old spots like clockwork. It looked as though business was booming. Not too long ago, he thought he'd never miss the game, but now he'd give anything to have a piece of the action.

Without Halleigh's knowledge, Malek had made a trip back to Flint, first to put Mitch in check, and secondly, to observe his old business. He thought about his woman, who waited at home for him miles away, thinking that their life was peachy. She didn't know they'd just hit rock bottom, and he was still trying to figure out a way so she'd never have to know.

How did I let this bullshit happen to me? Malek scolded himself. He knew the only person he could really be mad at was himself. He'd turned over his livelihood and put his trust in virtual strangers. When he thought about it, what did he really know about Gary anyway? He'd put in so much work to save the money, and then let some fast-talking guy sweet-talk him out of all of it, like a virgin on prom night being sweet-talked out of her panties by the prom king.

"Gary is a dirty mu'fucka!" Malek spat, shaking his head. *That's probably not even his real name.* When he got some money, he would figure out a

way to find him. *When I catch him, I'ma make him suffer.*

Malek looked at himself through the rearview mirror and felt pure failure and disgust. As he was beating himself up verbally with a string of expletives, he saw Mitch pull in front of the dope house in a blue Benz. Malek knew Mitch would be on his p's and q's, since he had caught him slipping but didn't kill him. He almost wished he hadn't given the fool a heads-up. But his anger had been in control as he did ninety miles per hour down the highway in the middle of the night to get at him.

Now, seeing the arrogant bastard rolling as if he really was boss, it took all of Malek's willpower not to step out of his car and blast that fool. He knew it wasn't the right time, though. Malek knew he was outnumbered, as Mitch was accompanied by some of his goons. So, he just sat there and watched as they disappeared into the house. Now his thoughts of revenge were aimed toward Mitch, and it was the only thing on Malek's mind. Oh, by no means did he plan on letting Gary get away with stealing from him, but right now a bird in the hand was worth two in the bush.

With Mitch refusing to let him back in the game, Malek was powerless. Nevertheless, with a baby on the way and a woman to take care of, Malek needed money. He came up with a plan. He was going to hit Mitch where it hurt the most. In the pockets.

I'ma hit all of his dope spots and take him for all he got. Malek glanced down at the pistol that sat in his lap. He knew his idea was not well thought out, but he was in extreme circumstances. The last time Malek called himself going to commit a robbery, his life went downhill after that. But the past was the past. Then he was a "virgin" on the streets, and it was his first time testing the waters. Now with his well-cultivated skills, he knew he had a better chance of pulling it off.

Malek wasn't no dummy, though. Having been away from the streets for a while, it was very possible that Mitch had changed up some things, so he needed someone who knew the ins and outs of the spots so he could rob them smoothly. That's where Malek's first problem surfaced. He had no idea who would know about Mitch's spots that wasn't loyal to him.

Malek noticed a man walking down the street with a 1980s pimp stroll, wearing raggedy clothes and a brown top hat with a feather. Although the man looked like a bum, his walk blared confidence. Upon closer observation, Malek realized it was Scratch, an old friend of Jamaica Joe.

A bulb went off in Malek's head. He knew right then and there that Scratch could be just as valuable to him as he'd been to Jamaica Joe. No matter what, Scratch always seemed to know any and everything that was going on in the streets, and always willingly reported the goings-on to Jamaica Joe.

Chapter Fourteen

"So are you game, old-timer?" Malek asked, his eye on the people going in and coming out of the dope house.

"Let me get this right." Scratch rubbed his hands together and thought long and hard about the opportunity Malek had just presented him. "Say, you want Scratch to help you rob Mitch's spots? I mean, I'm not a young gun like yo'self anymore. Scratch can't move like he used to, ya dig? Maybe I'm not the one you need to be recruiting for this here job."

When Malek first stopped Scratch as he made his way to the homeless shelter, Scratch thought he was about to get robbed.

"Yo," Malek called out, doing a light jog toward him, "hold up, my man."

Scratch had immediately raised his hands in surrender. "Look, youngblood, I ain't got noth-

ing for you. You got the wrong one. If you trying to stick me up, you'd just be practicing, because I'm on my way to the homeless shelter." Scratch nodded toward the shelter, which was only a few buildings ahead, making it a point to look straight ahead and not in Malek's eyes. He didn't want the young cat to kill him just because he'd witnessed his face, nor did he want him to think he was trying to challenge him.

"You got it all wrong, fam," Malek told him. "I'm not here to try to take something from you. As a matter of fact, I'm here to offer you something—the same way you used to always offer my man Jamaica Joe something."

Malek's words got Scratch's attention—especially the mention of Jamaica Joe's name. Scratch could recall the many times Jamaica Joe had broken him off some dough just for keeping his ears and eyes glued to the streets, so he assumed this kid wanted something similar from him.

Scratch lowered his hands and faced Malek. That's when he noticed the familiarity of Malek's face. "Hey, I know you. You used to run with Joe, his little prodigy or something. You was that kid that was supposed to go pro. You were supposed to be the American dream for all the people stuck in Flint, the example that there was a way out besides death or jail."

Malek should have been flattered at Scratch's words, but they only twisted the knife that he al-

ready felt was in his chest. Hearing that so many in the streets of Flint had put him on such a pedestal that his success would be a reflection of theirs only made him feel worse about his current predicament.

Seeing the blank look on Malek's face, Scratch continued, "So you said you got something for Scratch?" Like Malek, he knew that nothing in the streets came without a price. So now he'd just have to hear the youngster out and see if what he had to offer was worth it. "Talk to me, youngblood."

Scratch listened intently as Malek explained to him how he needed his assistance in seeing through his plan to rob Mitch's spots, and how after doing so, he could probably afford his own place rather than relying on the homeless shelter. Malek made it sound like an offer that Scratch couldn't refuse. "C'mon, man. You wanna spend the rest of your life sleeping in the homeless shelter? You help me with this, you won't have to worry about having money to get your own place." In all truth, Malek needed Scratch to keep him and his family from the homeless shelter.

"You're the perfect person for the job, actually." Malek could tell that Scratch was now seriously considering the proposal he'd hit him with. Malek turned toward Scratch, looking him directly into his eyes. "You know where all the spots are at. You can get in and peep the scene

for me, ya know? You can let me know how many workers are in the spot and where the straps are at."

Scratch thought for a moment before replying. "No disrespect, youngblood, but I never cut you out to be a stickup kid. You and Jamaica Joe were tight. I thought y'all were cut from the same cloth, but a stickup kid Joe was not. So, if you don't mind me asking, why are you hitting his old spots? Seems like, if anything, you'd be on the same team as his crew."

"Shit happens," Malek told him. "I was on the same team. It was me who Jamaica Joe handed the operation over to, not Mitch. But eventually, I handed it over to Mitch. My intentions were to leave the streets alone, you know."

Scratch could empathize with Malek. That was his intention as well, to leave the streets alone. "So you've changed your mind?"

"No. More like, some things that went down didn't really allow me a choice. But that's beside the point. What matters is that when I called up Mitch, the mu'fucka who I put on, and asked him for one small favor, he forgot that I was the one that put him in the position of power. So if he wants to play it that way, I'ma take instead of asking," Malek said, getting angrier with every word that came out of his mouth.

Scratch nodded his head, completely understanding the game. He was once the head dope man in his heyday, so he knew where Malek was

coming from. When he was on top, everybody wanted a piece of Scratch, but just as soon as he began to decline, no one wanted to reach out a helping hand. All they wanted to do was stick out a foot and kick him hard while he was down.

"I tell ya, youngblood, shit ain't like it used to be. I was in the game when it began to change. These young cats nowadays have no loyalty. That's the difference between the game back then and the game now. These young'uns in the game playing fo' keeps."

"So you game?" Malek asked, trying not to beat around the bush any longer. He felt like he'd shared enough information with Scratch for him to be able to make a decision on whether he was down. "Like I said before, if you're in, then I'll definitely hit you with something for your help. And if all really goes well, I'll make sure to hit you off with a li'l somethin'-some-thin'."

Scratch already knew what Malek was think-ing, and he wanted to let it be known that he was flying straight. "It ain't like that, man. Scratch left that bullshit alone. Like yourself, young-blood, Scratch trying to leave these streets and everything they stand for alone."

"Then we can say fuck these streets for the last time together. But we need each other to do it. Some things we just can't do by ourselves, and some things we do ain't just for ourselves. I got a

woman at home, and her future lies in my hands."

Malek's words jogged Scratch's memory. He remembered that Halleigh had expressed how crazy she was over Malek, and now he wondered if she was the woman at home he was referring to.

"Say, have you seen Halleigh?"

Malek saw the way Scratch's eyes lit up when he mentioned her name. At first he couldn't figure out why this crackhead would be so interested in knowing about his girl, but then it dawned on him exactly who Scratch was. He had been so caught up in his one-track mind, trying to get revenge on Mitch, he'd forgotten that Halleigh had explained to him how tight she and Scratch were.

Now Malek's eyes lit up. This was just one more thing he could use to his advantage. If Scratch wouldn't do it for Malek, then maybe he would do it for Halleigh. But Malek would only pull that ace out of the deck as a last resort. He needed to make sure he could trust Scratch. Once upon a time, Jamaica Joe trusted him very much, but like Scratch had just said, the game changes, and he had no way of knowing if Scratch had changed.

"Oh yeah. Halleigh is doing good," Malek answered. "I got her set up out of town."

Scratch smiled. He felt better, knowing Halleigh was doing okay. "So that's why no one

on the streets has seen her. Man, I been searching for her high and low. I need to get with her on some personal things."

Malek shot Scratch a quizzical look. He wondered why Scratch was so anxious to get at Halleigh. The only personal things those two ever had in common was dope. No matter how broke Malek got, he would never put Halleigh in a situation where she could go back to doing drugs.

As if Scratch could read the expression on Malek's face, he replied, "Youngblood, I told you I don't mess with drugs no more. It's not even like that. Li'l Rina is like a daughter to me. I would never . . ." Scratch's words trailed off. He couldn't finish his sentence without lying. Had it not been for him, Halleigh would have never gotten hooked in the first place.

Mistaking Scratch's sudden loss of words for him getting emotional and being sincere, Malek replied, "I tell you what. You help me, and I will take you to Halleigh. We got a deal?" Even if Malek didn't trust Scratch one hundred percent, he trusted Halleigh to make all the right decisions concerning her body and the health of their baby. After all, that was the reasoning he'd fed himself for the move he was about to make. It wasn't for him; it was for Halleigh and the baby.

"We got a deal," Scratch said without thinking twice. He extended his hand to Malek. With

everything Halleigh had done for him in the past, showing him undivided loyalty, providing inspiration throughout his recovery at the rehab center, he owed everything to her. If helping Malek was going to put her in a good place financially, then Scratch was all for it. Maybe after she found out that he helped, she'd listen to him, and then he could reunite her with Sharina. Then, in Scratch's mind, everything would be right with the world.

Malek shook Scratch's hand, and at that moment a partnership was formed, both sides offering something. Scratch was helping Malek seek revenge, and although he didn't know it, Malek was helping Scratch seek redemption. Malek only hoped that this partnership was the real deal.

"It's not going to be that simple, young-blood," Scratch said, keeping it real with the young'un. "Since Mitch and Sweets came together, they—"

"Sweets and Mitch? Together? What the fuck you talking about?" Malek's heart began pounding almost out of his chest, and his temperature began to rise.

"Well, from what I hear from the streets, Mitch and Sweets ended the North versus South beef to become one. It's all the same operation now. So you gotta know that if you hit Mitch, you also dabbling into Sweets' money," Scratch explained. "They got a lot of loyal cats up under them. You'd

be starting a one-man war against two teams. And I know you done seen the movie *300*. Though them soldiers put up a good fight, they lost in the end." Scratch was reminding him of the brutal outcome of the movie, in which the little army with a big heart got slain. In so many words, Scratch was trying to let him know that a big heart couldn't defeat a big army. Maybe in the olden days of the Bible it was possible, but not in the street game.

Malek had to get out of there. If he stood there any longer, he was liable to say the hell with a robbery and just straight-out get to poppin' off that lead. "Look, let's ride," Malek ordered Scratch, turning away and heading toward his car.

Scratch followed, and they got in his car, where Scratch continued to discuss the beef between the two sides of town. Malek was even more furious at that point. Not only did Mitch betray Malek, but he had sided with the person who killed Jamaica Joe. Mitch was playing a dirty game, and Malek hated it.

That nigga has no morals, Malek thought as he pulled away from the block.

Scratch said, "Can I ask you something, youngblood?"

Malek nodded his head, maneuvering through the city traffic.

"Have you ever done this before?" Scratch asked, referring to robbery.

"No. Can't be that hard, though, right?"

"It's time for ol' Scratch to give you a crash course in this game here we like to call robbery." Scratch remembered the days when he'd resorted to being a stickup kid to get high. He remembered the year that he and a heroin addict–turned street lit writer robbed the dope houses throughout Detroit, Flint, and Saginaw in the late '70's. "You can't run before you walk, youngblood. We need to hit Detroit before we just bust up into one of Mitch's spots."

"What you mean, Detroit?"

"We need a little practice, ya know. Now, you may no longer reside in the city limits, but I live here in Flint. I can't just shit where I sleep, unless I know there's enough toilet paper on the roll to wipe up all the mess." Scratch got situated and turned slightly to face Malek. "I've been shooting dope since before you was born, and in my journey, I have run across many dope houses throughout the state. We need to hit one that's not so close to home first, to get your game up," Scratch said, beginning to feel more comfortable.

As far as Scratch was concerned, robbing dope houses was like riding a bike. It was something a person never forgets how to do once they learn how. But he still needed to go for a test-ride, especially now that he had a sidekick. In his day, Scratch had never needed an accomplice.

As Scratch schooled Malek, he felt like his old self in his old habitat. "If we gonna do it, we gotta do it right." He flipped down Malek's mirror and fixed his brim. Then he winked at himself and declared, "Scratch is back!"

Chapter Fifteen

Halleigh sat in her living room reflecting on her life. She looked at the table, where Malek had left the note for her when he'd made his exit in the middle of the night. It read:

> *Good morning, Love*
> *Here's some money to go shopping and relax for the day. I'm going back into the city to handle some business, and I'll be home to you later tonight.*
> *Malek*

Along with the note was a stack of money that amounted to five thousand dollars, half of what Malek had left to his name. Every other time he'd given her money to hit the mall, it had never been anything less than that. He wanted to be consistent, to make sure that Halleigh didn't suspect anything regarding his recent loss. He

wanted to carry the burden and handle it on his own. Besides, he didn't plan on coming back home broke.

Halleigh was at a happy stage and was elated that her life was finally coming together. She had a good man, a baby on the way, and a beautiful home—out of Flint. Falling back onto the couch in what felt like the lap of luxury, she imagined that this was what Marie must feel like.

Thoughts of Marie caused Halleigh to pick up her cell phone and call the long-distance friend. She hadn't talked to her but once since returning from the island, and now was the perfect time to call her. With five Gs to spend, she hoped the classy Marie could give her some contacts for her next big purchase. Halleigh wanted to buy a diamond bracelet, and recalled Marie mentioning that she knew some jewelers in the Midwest with flawless diamonds for reasonable prices.

I know she knows someone, Halleigh thought as she held the phone to her ear.

When the call connected, she heard an unexpected recording at the other end. "This number is no longer in service. Please check the telephone number and try again."

Halleigh frowned and looked at her phone to make sure she was dialing the right number. The number was correct. "Her phone is turned off?" Halleigh said to herself, slightly confused.

Her game all fucked-up. She got a millionaire for a boyfriend and she can't keep her phone on? I'ma have

to teach her a thing or two. Halleigh flipped down her phone and got up so she could get dressed.

"I guess I'll go ahead and do a little bit of shopping today," she said as she headed into the back room.

Halleigh opened her robe and let it fall to the floor as she walked into the bathroom and turned on the shower. As she stepped beneath the spray, she dropped her hand to her stomach and smiled, thinking about the life forming inside of her. She adjusted the water temperature, and the steam began to fog up the room. Halleigh let the water hit her face and cascade down her body. The feeling of the hot water was almost orgasmic. She closed her eyes and was enjoying herself as images of Malek popped into her head.

Halleigh was so deep in thought that she didn't hear the two masked men creep into the bathroom with her. All of a sudden, she felt a cold draft as the shower doors flung open. Startled, Halleigh opened her eyes and found herself staring into the eyes of a man with a ski mask. She tried to scream, hoping Malek would somehow come and save her, but the man grabbed her and put a rag over her nose and mouth. She could smell the chloroform. She tried to kick and scream, to release herself from the man's grasp, but his strength was too much for her.

After only a few seconds of trying to free herself from the man's hold, Halleigh began to lose her consciousness. The foggy bathroom made

the scene dreamlike, leaving Halleigh disoriented and scared just before she finally blacked out.

A couple hours later, Halleigh woke up groggy, and still naked, the way she was when she was yanked out of the shower. She looked around the unfamiliar empty room. There was nothing in it, except for a toilet and a soiled mattress on the floor.

Confusion and fear sank in and Halleigh began to do the first thing she could think of doing and the last thing she remembered trying to do—scream for help. "Help! Somebody, help me!" She stood up and ran to the steel door, the only exit in the windowless room. She figured she was in a basement because of the concrete walls and floor. The moist air had a damp, horrendous smell that made her nauseated. She pounded on the door, screaming and kicking.

After a couple minutes of no response, she dropped to her knees in defeat. She began to think about her unborn baby as she gripped her stomach. *Oh my God! Who would do this? Where am I?*

"Malek, where are you?" she whispered, curling up into a fetal position and crying her eyes out.

* * *

"Here it is right here." Scratch pointed at the big brick house on Nebraska Avenue. He had taken Malek to a small weed spot that the local Mexicans ran on the east side of Detroit. "They move heavy reefer out of this one right here," Scratch said as he and Malek looked on.

"How you know?" Malek asked, wondering how a dopefiend knew about a weed spot. "Man, I know everything that goes on in this city," Scratch said with pride. "They've been making good money over here for years. Big Poncho is over this one, and he runs a solo operation. He sells weed out the front and a small amount of smack out the back. He has a shooting gallery in his basement. He charges dopeheads to come use his gallery, and it's small, but this spot will give us practice."

Scratch looked at the house and shook his head. "Whew! I ain't did this in years, young-blood," There was a little nervousness in his voice.

His adrenaline began to pump as he continued filling Malek in on the spot. "He might have a couple of li'l niggas in there, but nothing serious. If we do it right, we can hit him and take him for what he got. He keeps his money under floorboards in the closet in the master bedroom.

"You say he doesn't have a lot of people around him?"

"That's right. Sometimes his little brother is

in there with him, and sometimes his li'l honey dips, but for the most part, he never has a crew inside. But he does keep a gun on his hip at all times, and I know he probably has a couple of straps stashed around the house."

Malek sat and listened intently as he put a plan together in his mind. *Maybe Scratch isn't as dumb as he looks.*

"I got a plan," Malek said as he cocked his gun back. He reached into his glove box, pulled out another pistol, and set it in Scratch's lap.

Scratch gripped the gun and examined it like it was a rare art piece. He cocked it back also, loving the way the cold steel felt in his palms. It had been years since he held a gun, and it felt damn good.

After Scratch finished schooling Malek on the scenario, the two got out of the car and prepared to proceed with their plan. Malek kneeled by a bush near Poncho's back door, waiting for Scratch to unlock the back door for his entry. Scratch had gone into the house through the front door with the intent to let Malek in.

As Malek waited, it felt as though hours had gone by. He was beginning to think Scratch had chickened out. "I know I shouldn't have dealt with a junkie," he whispered as he remained in a crouched position. He gripped his black .45 and stared at the door. Then, he heard the sound of the back door being unlocked. Malek smiled. Scratch had held up his end of the plan.

But just as Malek rose and walked to the door, he saw something unexpected. A Mexican-looking female with long, flowing hair came walking out the door with a garbage bag, apparently to take out the trash.

They locked eyes and stared at each other in silence. When the girl saw that Malek was wearing all black and a ski mask rolled up on top of his head, she figured out he wasn't there for a friendly get-high visit. She tried to run back into the house, but Malek grabbed her by the hair and put his gun in her face.

"Shhh!" he ordered, quieting her before she even got the chance to scream for help. "Look, if you listen and do everything I tell you to do, then you won't get hurt," Malek said sternly. "But I promise you, if you make one false move . . ." Malek didn't see the need to finish his sentence.

The girl nodded and began to tear up. Malek guided her back into the house as he pulled his ski mask over his face. He put his gun to the back of the girl's head and pressed her into the living room, where Poncho was weighing up ounces of weed.

Poncho was taken by surprise. Malek pushed the girl toward him. Poncho tried to grab his gun, which was on the coffee table near him, but Malek swiftly motioned toward him, causing him to freeze.

"Don't try it!" Malek pointed the gun directly at his head.

Poncho instantly put up his hands and swore under his breath, knowing he'd been caught slipping.

"You already know what time it is, homeboy. Where the stash at?" Malek walked closer to him and put the gun to his temple. He cautiously looked around the room, making sure that no one caught him slipping, and hoping Scratch would surface.

Once again, he kicked himself for thinking he could trust a junkie. He was certain that thoughts of their plan had gone right out of Scratch's mind the minute he walked into the dope house.

"There isn't a stash, bro," Poncho said with a heavy Spanish accent.

"Oh, so you think I'm playing, huh?" Malek smirked. Without hesitation, he pointed the gun at Poncho's foot and let out a shot, leaving Poncho's Timberland boot smoking and pouring blood. Poncho's and the girl's screams echoed through the house as Malek watched him roll around on the floor in agony.

At that point, Malek was going for broke. He didn't care how he got money. His only concern was taking care of Halleigh and his child, and if niggas had to suffer for the happiness of his loved ones, so be it.

"So let's try this again. Where is the stash?" Malek said, more authority in his tone this time.

The girl didn't even let Poncho respond. She pointed to the back room and yelled, "It's all in

the back safe, under the floorboards." She was crying hysterically.

Poncho knew he had to kiss his whole stash good-bye. "Stupid bitch!"

Malek smiled. He was about to tie them up, but before he got to Poncho, he felt a gun on the back of his neck and froze up. He slowly raised his hands, not wanting to turn around and cause Poncho's younger brother to shoot.

The gunman, his red bandana covering his forehead and sitting right above his eyes, said, "You fucked with the wrong *ese*, homes! Drop the gun!" He nudged Malek with the barrel of the shotgun.

Before Malek could obey the man's command, another familiar voice filled the air, a more smooth tone. "Naw, playa, *you* might wanna drop your gun." Scratch pressed his gun to the back of the man's head.

Malek smiled. Scratch had come through for him.

"Drop it!" Scratch yelled.

Poncho's younger brother dropped his gun and put his hands up. Poncho continued to shake his head, regretting that he wasn't more cautious. He couldn't believe that a junkie had set him up to be robbed.

Malek grabbed Poncho off the floor and guided him to the back. "Scratch, hold it down in here!" Malek yelled before he exited the living room with Poncho.

"I gotcha, youngblood." Scratch kept his gun

trained on the woman and Poncho's younger brother, while Malek went back to get the money. Scratch smiled, feeling good to be a part of something. It gave him a sense of importance, and while the ride lasted, he was definitely enjoying it.

Chapter Sixteen

A small smile formed on Mitch's face as he sat in one of his many stash houses and watched Halleigh on the monitor. She was balled up on the ground, crying. He, along with his henchman, Bugz, shared a weed-filled blunt while watching her like she was a star on a television reality show. Mitch had had a camera installed in the basement room where he held Halleigh.

Bugz smiled as he enjoyed every minute of the torture Halleigh was going through. He was tall and lanky with a neat Caesar haircut. Two huge front teeth had earned him the name Bugz, because of his close resemblance to the cartoon character, Bugs Bunny.

"How long are we going to keep her down there?" Bugz asked after he exhaled the weed smoke.

"As long as we need to. That nigga Malek

thinks shit is sweet. He should have killed me when he had a chance. Now I'ma make that nigga suffer," Mitch said as he saw flashbacks of Malek holding the gun to his head.

He knew Halleigh was Malek's weakness, and the best way to get back at him. It wasn't hard for him to get Malek's address. He had a computer geek on his team that could find out any information that he needed about Malek, so finding where he rested his head at was simple.

Mitch stood up and began to think about how he was going to kill Malek once he got to him. The only thing he had to do now was to wait. He was expecting a call from Malek sometime soon.

"I'm not going to just kill him. I'm going to make that nigga regret the day he woke up and thought he could put a gun in my face. I am the new king of Flint. Hands down!" Mitch yelled as he paced the room and his rage began to take over.

Malek and Scratch bolted out of the house with two bags full of weed and money. They left the three Mexicans gagged and tied up. Malek popped the trunk and tossed the goods inside while Scratch hopped in the passenger's seat. Malek snatched the mask off of his face and got in the driver's side and pulled off.

"That's what I'm talking about, youngblood!" Scratch said excitedly. "I haven't had that type of

rush in years." He looked back at the house in his rearview mirror. "This shit was supposed to go down. Can you believe not another mu'fucka was up in that house?"

Malek was just as excited as Scratch that the two had pulled off the robbery, even though things hadn't gone exactly as planned. "Good job, Scratch," Malek said as he maneuvered the car through traffic.

"Thanks, youngblood. Scratch still got it, baby," Scratch said, talking to himself more than Malek.

"That's not the hit I wanted, though. This can't be any more than ten thousand in cash and about fifty grand worth of bullshit weed that probably won't even sell," Malek said, slightly frustrated but not completely ungrateful. The only thing on his mind was getting back the money that Gary had swindled from him. He would go after Gary later, but until that could happen, he had to make sure he had enough money to support Halleigh in the way he'd promised. There would be no scraping to buy groceries for his family.

"See, youngblood, this wasn't for the money. This was practice for the big hit. You did a lot of things wrong, and if that was one of Mitch's or Sweets' spots, you would have been dead."

Malek frowned up at Scratch's comment, not liking the fact that Scratch was pointing out his flaws. But something in Malek told him that he

should listen to what the old G was saying. Wisdom was something no one could buy, so he allowed Scratch to continue without interference.

"The first mistake was, you didn't keep everything in front of you," Scratch told him. "You gave the other cat room to sneak up on you. You have to work from a corner, so that nothing can creep up behind you."

Malek knew Scratch was correct. "Is that right?"

"That's right. Another thing you did was underestimate the female. You had your gun just on Poncho, and all your attention was on him. If that fox was smart and up on the game, she could have popped you with the gun that was hid in the seat of the couch. I guess she didn't know it was there, but Scratch peeped it as soon as he got in the room."

Malek listened close and soaked up the game that Scratch was dropping. Although Scratch was a raggedy has-been in the street game, there was definitely knowledge there that he had picked up through his rough journey. Malek was new to the stickup game. He only knew how to hustle and move bricks; but he was a quick learner, and now he had his sights set on Mitch's spots.

Malek thought about his former comrade's complete disloyalty and disrespect. "I'm ready to get at Mitch," he said under his breath.

"I don't wanna throw a wrench in your program, youngblood, but if you wanna hit Mitch, you might want to go in the middle of the morning. That way you can catch him unsuspecting. If

we go now, he's gonna have young guns sitting around, waiting to pop off."

Malek nodded and got on the highway. "You right."

"So, if it ain't too much, can I see my girl Halleigh now? Scratch ain't seen her in a while," Scratch said like a proud father.

"I got you, baby," Malek said as he headed toward their home in Grand Blanc. He knew the close relationship that Halleigh and Scratch had. After all, he was the reason why she'd been at the rehab center during the shooting. He usually wouldn't bring anybody to his home, but he would make an exception for Scratch. He felt that Halleigh would appreciate being surprised by Scratch's presence.

"Just don't say nothin' to her about what we just did, okay?" Malek warned.

"No doubt," Scratch answered then leaned back in the seat, happy he was going to see his girl, Li'l Rina.

Chapter Seventeen

Bugz watched Halleigh closely on the screen. Mitch had left to make a couple runs and had assigned him to stay at the abandoned stash house with her, so he was responsible for feeding and guarding her. Bugz watched as Halleigh kicked and screamed, trying to get help. The more he looked at her, the more he became fascinated by her.

Mitch was very adamant about telling Bugz not to mistreat or even interact with Halleigh while she was in their custody, explaining to him that she wasn't the enemy, just a means to an end. But Halleigh's beauty was too much for Bugz to resist. He looked at her curvaceous body and wondered what it would be like to have a woman of her beauty. Her perky breasts and fat ass had him aroused, and he wanted to feel the inside of her. Although her hair was wild and she was distraught, she still was beautiful in his eyes.

Actually, he had gone to school with Halleigh, but she became too popular and out of his reach once she hooked up with the so-called basketball star. She never gave him a second glance. He'd always had a small crush on her and secretly envied Malek. Now that the tables were turned and her life was in his hands, it was sweet revenge for him.

He walked over to the refrigerator, grabbed a TV dinner, and tossed it in the microwave. He waited for it to warm and then headed down the basement stairs with it.

Halleigh heard the creaking of the wooden stairs, and her heart began to beat fast. She didn't know who to expect to walk into the room, and hurried to the corner, as far away from the door as possible. She sat down and pulled her knees close to her chest as she waited to see who was coming. She heard the dead bolts being unlocked—there were at least four of them on the door.

Halleigh saw the tall, lean man step into the room. She began to breathe heavily as she stared at the face that had some familiarity to it. "Where the fuck am I?" she asked, trying to figure out how she knew the guy.

"Don't worry about it." Bugz tossed the TV dinner toward Halleigh then slowly approached her. As he got closer, he could see Halleigh tense up, trying to cover her naked body with her hands as best she could. Bugz was in awe at her physique.

"I'm not going to hurt you," he said as he stood over her.

She looked up at him and screamed, "Why in the fuck am I here? Why?"

"Look, I don't know why. I'm just—"

Before Bugz could finish his sentence, Halleigh gave him a power punch to his groin, sending intense pain through his body.

"Aghhh!" he yelled as he grabbed his nuts and bent over in agony.

Halleigh made a run for it. She jumped up and bolted, darting up the stairs, where she tried to open the door. It was locked. She pounded on it furiously and screamed for help, but it was to no avail.

Bugz limped to the bottom of the stairs and looked up at Halleigh, who was hollering and trying her best to open the door. "You can't go anywhere without these, bitch." He held up a set of keys that unlocked the dead bolts on both doors.

"Let me go, you sick bastard!" Halleigh screamed as she glanced down at him. Then she began to pound on the door again. She wanted so desperately for her man to come and save her and her baby.

She wondered why this man had her locked up in basement in the first place. Who would want to do this to her? At first she couldn't imagine. But then one person in particular popped into her mind—Manolo. Maybe he had something to do with this.

"You can bang on the door as long as you want and scream as loud as you want, but nobody can hear you. You might as well come back down here, sit yo ass down here, and eat this food," Bugz said, massaging his aching balls. "That was a good shot you got on me, but if you do it again, I'm not gonna take it so lightly." He pulled out his gun; then he grabbed the shirt that was hanging out of his back pocket and threw it at her. "Cover yourself up and come back down here."

Halleigh gripped her stomach, thinking about the safety of her baby. She picked up the shirt that landed at her feet and put it on. Realizing she had no choice but to abide by his rules, she walked down the stairs and hesitantly approached Bugz.

When she got close to him, he grabbed her by the hair and threw her back into the room. She fell on her side and quickly headed to the corner, trying to get as far away from him as she could.

Bugz was enjoying watching Halleigh suffer. He wanted to have a little fun with her. "Now, let's try this again," he said with a menacing smirk. He was about to take what she would never give to him willingly.

Chapter Eighteen

Malek and Scratch reached the house. But-
terflies formed in Scratch's stomach as he
prepared to see Halleigh. He was happy he would
finally be able to talk to her again, because he
missed his friend, but also because he wanted to
convince her to forgive her mother. He hoped it
would mean something to Halleigh that her
mother had finally gotten clean and was one
hundred percent drug-free.

"Halleigh is gonna be happy to see you," Malek
said as he approached his front door.

Scratch followed closely. He took off his hat
and tried his best to pat down his nappy 'fro.
"Gotta look good for my girl," he said to himself
as he tried to straighten up his 1980s-looking
shirt.

Malek put the key in the door and noticed it
was unlocked. "I told that girl about not locking
up," he said as he pushed open the door. "We

may not be in Flint, but hell, crime don't discriminate." He smiled as he raised the duffel bags containing the money and the weed. He was going to split everything from their caper down the middle with Scratch. It wasn't nearly enough to set him up financially, but it would help. He knew the big heist would be at Mitch's and Sweets' spots.

Malek walked into the house and called for Halleigh. "Hal, come out, baby. I have a surprise for you." He dropped the bags in the middle of the floor and headed toward the back room.

Scratch sat on the couch and made himself comfortable. He looked around and admired the plush place. It had been a while since he had been in a home so nice.

Moments later, Malek came storming out the back, his gun drawn and a note in his hand.

Scratch saw the look of worry written all over Malek's face. "What's wrong, youngblood?"

"Man, they got Halleigh!"

"What?" Scratch jumped up, not knowing exactly what was going on.

"I'ma kill that nigga!" Malek dropped the note on the table.

Scratch picked up the note and read the sloppy handwriting: *If you want to see your whore again, come see me. If you try that brave shit, she's dead. Mitch.*

"Damn!" Scratch dropped his head and shook it from side to side.

"This ain't for her. This is not for her, man,"

Malek said as he thought about the love of his life and how he put her in harm's way. She'd already had a rough life, and he was making it worse. The burden of guilt rested on his shoulders, and then the thought of his unborn child came into play.

Malek got teary-eyed and began to clench his jaws and fists. He looked around and noticed a lamp on the floor and the phone off the hook. There must have been a struggle when they took Halleigh, and the thought of it made him even more furious. He headed for the door, willing to sacrifice his life to make sure Halleigh and their child would be okay.

Scratch followed Malek out without thinking twice. He was ready to ride or die for Halleigh. They were on their way straight to Mitch's main "trap spot."

Chapter Nineteen

Mitch, surrounded by his goons, was in his main trap spot in the 5th Ward. He was smoking a blunt at a table where ounces of coke sat in piles, ready to be cooked up for distribution. He was waiting for Malek to enter any minute. He knew he would be on his way, because Malek had been calling him constantly. But Mitch didn't want to talk over the phone; he wanted to tell him what he had to say to his face.

He felt bad for kidnapping Halleigh, but in his eyes, it was all a part of the game. Mitch was a strong believer in an eye for an eye, and Malek had violated.

Mitch still had a thing for Halleigh, and he had no intentions of hurting her. In fact, he always wanted to be in Malek's shoes when it came to Halleigh. That was a contributing factor to his disloyalty. Just like he didn't think Malek had earned his way to the top of the game, he didn't

think Malek deserved Halleigh either. He smirked at the thought that once Malek was out of the picture, maybe he would make her his woman.

Just as expected, Malek stormed through the door, along with Scratch.

Mitch stood up and smiled at Malek, as if they were friends. "Oh shit! Look what we got here—Dumb and Dumber." He laughed. "What? You running with dopefiends now, son? Shit must be real bad, huh?"

He was the only one laughing. Malek was furious as he stood a few feet away from Mitch. All of Mitch's goons had their hands on their waists, by their guns, waiting for Malek to make the wrong move.

"I see you got my letter, huh?"

"Where is Halleigh?" Malek said through clenched teeth, cutting right to the chase. He stared at Mitch intensely, hatred in his eyes, and didn't blink once. He wanted to put a bullet through Mitch's skull right then and there.

Mitch had Halleigh, so he was in complete control. He pointed his finger in Malek's face. "I should be the one asking all the questions, my nigga. Pat this clown down."

Three men ran up on Malek and searched him. One of them found a gun in his waist and quickly gave it to Mitch.

"You can take me. Just let her go, man," Malek said, trying to reason with Mitch.

"How do you know she isn't already dead?" Mitch said, sending darts straight to Malek's heart.

The words made Malek's knees weak, but he stood firm.

Scratch had heard enough. He pulled out the gun Malek had given him and tried to point it toward Mitch. He handled the gun like an amateur, fumbling it, and Mitch's goons quickly attacked him and gave him a beatdown.

Two of Mitch's goons started striking Scratch on the head with their guns, causing blood to trickle down his face. Malek stood there helplessly as Scratch got beat down by the two men who were half his age.

"Let that bum up," Mitch ordered as they stomped out Scratch. The goons returned to Mitch's side and focused on Malek.

Scratch spat up blood and held his stomach in agony. He slowly got up, blood pouring from different gashes on his face and mouth; but he still managed to release his famous smile. "That's . . . all you . . . young punks got?" Scratch gasped and held his broken jaw.

Just as the words came out of Scratch's mouth, a goon gave him another hit for good measure, this time knocking him out cold.

Mitch looked at Malek and thought about how he ran up on him in his own house. He wanted to make him suffer before he eventually killed him.

"I got somebody I want you to meet." Mitch

looked toward the back room. "Yo!" he hollered, calling someone.

Moments later, Sweets, the homo thug responsible for the death of Jamaica Joe, emerged from the back. He crooned in a singsong voice, "Malek, Malek, Malek."

Just months ago, the two had been at each other's throats over a turf war, and now Malek was face to face with him. He thought he would never see Sweets anywhere on the North side of Flint. Mitch had sided with the enemy, which only made Malek feel more angry and betrayed.

"Fuck you, Sweets!"

Sweets sat nonchalantly at the table, buried his head in one of the blow piles, and used his nose as a vacuum. Then he threw his head back, smiling as he wiped his powdered nose. "No. Fuck *you!*" he said. "It looks like you have made yourself a li'l situation here," Sweets said, referring to Malek's beef with Mitch. "I would hate to be you right now," he said in an instigating tone. "Oh yeah, and just to let you know . . . I faithfully piss on Jamaica Joe's grave every day. You know, I got to keep the flowers watered. It helps them grow better."

Everyone in the room had a good laugh, except for Malek and Scratch, who was still out cold on the floor.

"Okay, okay, enough of the reunion. You thought you could get away with coming in my shit like that?" Mitch asked Malek.

Malek remained quiet, but stared at Mitch intensely.

Mitch, gun in hand, walked over to Malek and stood face to face with him. He lifted the gun and pressed it to Malek's lips. "Open up," he whispered.

Malek gritted his teeth and kept his mouth shut.

Mitch shouted the order again, this time cocking the gun, and Malek reluctantly opened his mouth. Mitch forced the barrel of the gun in.

Meanwhile, Scratch began to regain consciousness. He shook his head, trying to focus his blurred vision. Once he remembered what was going on, his only thoughts were to get Halleigh back. He sat and watched the situation unfold.

Mitch stood right in front of Malek. "I want a half-million in seventy-two hours," Mitch said, thinking about the dough that Malek had exited the drug game with. "If that money isn't in my hands by Friday, you can start picking out Halleigh's casket."

A rare tear slid down Malek's cheek. He thought about his woman. He had put her in harm's way, and hadn't been there when she needed him.

Mitch pushed Malek forcefully and smiled. "You better go get my money, bitch," he said, like a pimp talking to one of his hoes on a Saturday night. Mitch thought Malek had money put away, but little did he know, Malek was dead broke.

Scratch got up and followed Malek out the door. They had only three days to get a half-million dollars, which was next to impossible, considering any money Malek had planned on getting was from Mitch's spot. Malek had to do something to get his love back, and Scratch was going to do all he could to help. They had no plan and little hope.

Halleigh cried her eyes out in the corner as blood trickled down her leg. She ached all over after being raped by Bugz. Just when she thought her life was changing for the better, the streets of Flint had grabbed her. Now she was knee-deep in the game once again.

The shirt she wore had been ripped, and her eye was beginning to swell because of the blow he'd delivered to her when she tried to resist. She'd told Bugz she was pregnant while he was degrading her, but he didn't care. It only made him go harder, as if it excited him.

Bugz exited the room breathing heavily, a devilish smirk on his face. He finally got a piece of the "devil's pie."

Halleigh became lightheaded and nauseated, owing to the odor of semen and blood. Feeling herself starting to lose consciousness, she cried out for Malek. He'd broken his promise to never let anything else happen to her. Now, she hon-

estly didn't know if she could ever trust him again. The last thing that rolled off her tongue before she blacked out was Malek's name.

To be continued . . .

Flint Book 6:
A King is Born

Chapter One

Halleigh's body was racked with violent shivers as she hugged her knees close to her chest and tried to hide herself in the shadows of the dreary basement. She had just come to, having no idea exactly how long she'd been unconscious. For a second there she'd forgotten about what had taken place just moments before she blacked out, but when she looked down at her body, she was quickly reminded.

She looked around the room, her eyes darting from one corner to the next, almost as if she were on drugs; but drugs were a thing of the past. She had been perfectly drug-free for a long time. This act of paranoia came from the fact that she could feel someone watching her. Although no one appeared to be in the room with her, she could feel eyes burning through her.

After a few more moments of scanning the basement, she finally spotted what she could

sense was there: the eye of a camera. She could see the tiny red blink of a camcorder in the upper corner of the room. Once again, she felt violated. She reached out in an attempt to grab something to cover herself, but nothing was there. She had no choice but to resume her earlier position—knees to her chest, with her arms curled around her legs.

She rocked slowly until a sharp pain forced her to let out a gasp. That's when she recalled that she'd been bleeding ever since Bugz had violated her, and now she feared for her baby's life. She buried her face between her knees as tears fell from her eyes. She didn't want whoever was watching her to be empowered by her tears, so she felt the need to hide them.

She couldn't help but wonder if anybody had been watching her while she was being raped. Who had sat in front of the monitor and witnessed the horrible act without intervening? What type of person could do something like that? Whoever it was, she hated them. Their voyeuristic sin was cruel, and she was desperate for an escape.

Suddenly, Halleigh lifted her head as a memory flashed before her eyes. In the split second between her being snatched from the shower and a cloth being put over her nose and mouth, she'd looked into the bathroom mirror and saw something . . . someone. Someone familiar.

"Mitch?" the words fell off of her tongue as she realized that all of this was possibly his doing. "I

need to see Mitch," Halleigh whispered to herself.

If Mitch was behind this entire thing, she knew she had a chance to survive after all. As far as Halleigh knew, she'd never done anything to Mitch to prompt him to do something like this to her, so she could only assume that this had nothing to do with her at all, but everything to do with him and Malek. She didn't know what had sparked a beef between Mitch and Malek, but she did know that Mitch had been sweet on her at one point. She hoped that he still was. If so, perhaps she could use it to her advantage.

She knew that his attraction toward her was probably the only way she could ever get out of the situation alive, and she was willing to do whatever she had to in order to ensure her baby's safety.

Where are you, Malek? she asked herself as her eyes darted frantically around the room. She was trembling in fear. She didn't know what to expect next. It had been a full twenty-four hours since she had been given any food, and she hadn't seen another face besides Bugz's. The thought crossed her mind that now that Bugz had gotten what he wanted from her and she could identify who he was, she would be left for dead.

She shook her head in an attempt to erase those dreadful thoughts. She hoped and prayed that Bugz was gone for good, but that someone else would come see about her. Bugz wasn't in this alone; she knew that much. There had to be

someone else that had been assigned to keep guard over her, but who? Maybe her eyes had deceived her. Maybe it wasn't Mitch she'd seen before blacking out.

She closed her eyes and ran the scene through her mind; the scene that had happened so quickly. She visualized the shadowy figure that had stood off to the side, and unless her mind was deceiving her, it was indeed Mitch.

Opening her eyes, Halleigh wished to God this had all been just a bad dream, but the fact remained that she was still being held hostage. The torment of being locked in the basement reminded Halleigh of when Manolo had imprisoned her in his basement for weeks. It had been sheer torture, and she truly believed that a part of her had been forever locked in that basement. When she was finally released, she was a partial image of the person she used to be. She could only wonder what kind of emotions this time would bring upon her. How much of her soul would she leave behind this time, if she made it out at all?

Everything in Halleigh just wanted to get up, go beat on that door, and cry out for help, but she was all out of screams. There was no fight left in her. All she really wanted to do was just go home. She would do anything to be back home, safe and sound in her bed, next to her man.

She closed her eyes once again, and instantly, Malek's face appeared behind her lids. Her

heartbeat began to speed up as she thought about the possibility of never seeing him again.

She couldn't understand for the life of her why it seemed as though the two of them were always lingering on the edge. Why was it that their love was so hard to keep? Just when it appeared as though they'd picked themselves up and dusted themselves off again, they were being kicked back down. There was always something in their way, trying to keep them apart.

Perhaps, Halleigh thought, she and Malek simply were not supposed to be together. True love couldn't possibly be this hard to maintain, could it?

Tears ran down her face as she kept her eyes squeezed shut. She could see him smiling at her. He was holding her baby—their baby—in his arms. A sob escaped from her lips as she imagined Malek staring lovingly at her, rocking a baby boy back and forth in his arms. Halleigh had never seen that much joy in Malek's face, and she was mesmerized by the child he was holding. He was beautiful; the most beautiful baby boy she had ever seen. His smooth chocolate skin was flawless, and his big doe eyes were innocent and sweet. She fell in love at first sight, even if it was just a dream.

As quickly as she fell in love, grief took over. She saw Malek fall to his knees with the baby in his hands. A look of pain donned his face, and the front of his white T-shirt filled with crimson

blood. Halleigh reached out for him, but she couldn't get to him. She heard her baby crying, but she couldn't move. The only thing she could do was cry.

Halleigh's eyes shot open at the sight of her love dying, and she stared into space. "God, please help us," she pleaded.

She couldn't help but think that her vision was some type of premonition. *That's why he hasn't come for me yet,* she reasoned in her mind. *Please, God, let Malek be okay.* Her love for him was just that deep. Even while she was in distress, she prayed for his wellbeing. Even if a part of her was angry that he wasn't there for her, she still couldn't help but love him. They were soul mates, and her love for him was unselfish and unyielding. It was evident that no matter what, she couldn't force herself to not love that man. Only death itself could keep her from loving him. She hoped, though, that wouldn't be the case

Mitch entered the trap house, his authority causing his henchmen to straighten up and pretend as if they hadn't just been distracted by the game of NBA Live they'd been playing for some hours. Mitch stood in the living room in his Pelle jacket, black hoodie, and Sean John jeans, with a Styrofoam food box in his hand.

"Turn that bullshit off," Mitch stated in his low, serious tone. He walked over to the TV

monitors and looked at Halleigh on the screen. "She ate?"

"Nah," Bugz replied distractedly as he continued to play the game.

"Since when?" Mitch replied as he pulled his baggy pants up on his waistline.

"Shit, I don't know, man. Yesterday I think," Bugz replied, refusing to turn his attention away from the game.

"Why not?" Mitch asked calmly as he went over to where Bugz and two other corner boys were sitting.

"The bitch ain't got no act-right in her," Bugz said as he hit the blunt that was being passed around. He chuckled as he thought about his sexual tryst with the captive.

Mitch walked over to the game and snatched the cords out of the wall, interrupting their tournament. "Fuck am I paying you niggas for? Huh?" Mitch asked. "Didn't I give y'all strict orders? Why didn't y'all feed her? She's pregnant!"

Bugz frowned and shot back, "Damn, fam, I didn't know we was running a luxury hotel out this bitch. We kidnapped that broad. So, I forgot to feed her. I don't see why we hanging onto this bitch anyway. I say we pop her ass and pop that bitch-ass nigga Malek."

Mitch shook his head in disdain and then lunged at Bugz, hemming him up by his collar. He pointed a threatening finger in his face. "You feed her because I say feed her, nigga. I'm

boss. You don't need to know why we hanging onto her. I'm not paying you to be sitting around with these mu'fuckas glued to an X-box. Understand?"

Bugz snatched away from Mitch, embarrassed by the fact that he had been degraded in front of his peers, but he humbled himself and replied, "Yeah, I got you, fam." He brushed his shoulders off as if Mitch had gotten dirt on him by touching him. "Damn . . . my fault, my nigga. I'll go feed her now." Bugz headed toward the kitchen.

"I got it," Mitch said as he grabbed the food he had intended for himself and started down the stairs to give it to Halleigh. He mumbled to himself about how incompetent Bugz was as he made his way to the bottom of the steps.

The loud noise his Timberland boots made as he descended the steps sounded identical to Bugz's footsteps, and Halleigh cowered in fear, huddling farther into the corner of the basement.

As Mitch reached the bottom of the steps, he could see her through the darkness. He looked up and fumbled around before he pulled the string hanging from the ceiling to illuminate the room. A yellow glow shone throughout the basement, and a funky smell, like fresh blood, filled the air. Mitch immediately frowned up and walked toward Halleigh.

"Halleigh, come and grab some of this food," Mitch stated, his voice causing her to turn around.

"Mitch?" she called out weakly.

He didn't respond.

Halleigh blinked a couple of times, adjusting her eyes to the light. Once she could see clearly, it was evident that Mitch was the person in the basement with her, confirming that she had been right all along. He had been the second figure she'd seen after being snatched out of the shower.

"Mitch, please let me go. Why are you doing this to me?" she asked from the floor. She wanted to stand, but her body was in too much pain.

Mitch swallowed hard, coaching himself the entire time not to let Halleigh's sweet voice get to him. "Come eat," was all he said.

He squatted down near her and put the food on the floor. There was a look of terror in Halleigh's eyes, and Mitch tried his best to avoid eye contact with her as guilt bombarded his soul. The last thing he had ever wanted Halleigh to do was to look at him as though he was nothing but a monster. It definitely wasn't the same look he'd seen her give Malek. He'd secretly longed for that look, not the one he was receiving now.

As Mitch looked downward, dodging Halleigh's eyes, he noticed dried blood between her thighs. He could smell sex and sweat in the air. He frowned as he lifted her chin and rubbed her hair gently as if she was his woman.

Halleigh closed her eyes. She couldn't stand to look into his eyes like that. She could still feel him staring at her, though. She began to shake,

thinking that he, too, may force himself upon her.

He observed the torn shirt as well. Between that, the blood, and the smell, Mitch's hands began to shake as he put two and two together in his mind. His eyes scanned Halleigh once more. Her once confident swagger was replaced with fear and an insecurity that he hadn't seen in her since her days as a Manolo Mami. The blood on her thighs only confirmed his suspicions.

No wonder Bugz hadn't fed her. He was too busy trying to fuck her.

Son of a bitch! Mitch thought about his hard-headed, horny worker.

"Mitch, please . . ." Halleigh whispered, interrupting his thoughts. "I need to see a doctor. He raped me, Mitch. He hurt me real bad. I just need to make sure my baby is okay. That's all I want to do. Please, Mitch," Halleigh pleaded.

Mitch clenched his jaw and rose to his feet. He was too pissed for Halleigh's soft words to even penetrate him at that moment.

He emerged from the basement and stood near the door as he motioned for Bugz to approach him.

"Yeah, uh, what's up, fam?" Bugz stammered. He could tell by the menacing look on Mitch's face that Mitch wasn't too pleased with him. He'd already gotten on him about starving the poor girl, so certainly he was over that and on to something else.

"Why is she bleeding?" Mitch asked Bugz, staring him straight in the eyes as if daring him to try to lie.

Bugz attempted to laugh the tension away and answered, "I told you the bitch ain't got no act-right." Bugz grabbed his private parts. "So a nigga had to put some up in her." He snatched at his crotch obnoxiously and turned to walk away.

"Yo, Jake?" Mitch called out to one of the other henchmen sitting on the couch.

"What up?" Jake replied.

BOOM!

Out of nowhere, Mitch put a bullet through the back of Bugz's head. "Clean this mu'fucka up." Mitch glared from one corner boy to the other. "Any of you other niggas who can't follow orders gon' find yourself in the same predicament. I said watch her and feed her. Nothing more, nothing less." Mitch was furious at what had taken place in his absence.

The room was quiet, but Jake hopped up and did as he was told. He shook his head in shock as he began to dispose of the body, but he didn't dare say a word. He wasn't trying to see Mitch, and he definitely wasn't trying to be next.

Just as quickly as Mitch's temper had flared, it settled, and he went back into the basement. He removed the coat he was wearing and covered Halleigh's body before picking her up and carrying her up the stairs. Her body was limp in his arms, almost like a rag doll. She had no energy

to protest her relocation, and Mitch's arms provided her with warmth from his body heat.

Halleigh hadn't the slightest idea where Mitch could be taking her, but she didn't even have the energy to protest anyway. She had been in a damp basement and she knew that whatever he had in store for her couldn't be worse than that.

The first thing Halleigh saw when she emerged from the basement in Mitch's arms was Bugz's dead body on the floor. She looked up at Mitch, who simply stepped over the body without a word then carried her up another flight of stairs. He took her to a bedroom and laid her onto the queen size bed.

"Look, Halleigh, this wasn't supposed to happen," Mitch finally spoke. "This wasn't part of the plan."

"Plan?" Halleigh asked with a puzzled look on her face. "What plan, Mitch? What's going on?"

Refusing to allow the tenderness in Halleigh's voice to get to him, Mitch ignored her queries and continued speaking. "I'ma call a friend of mine over here to check on you and make sure you and your baby are okay." He deliberately put some sternness and bass into his voice to let Halleigh know that even though he was about to get her some help, he still meant business. "Don't act a fucking fool up in here either, screaming and all that. Don't give me a reason to hurt you, Halleigh. I don't want to take it there with you, so don't leave me without a choice. Just chill out

for a minute, and at the end of all this, you will walk out of here unharmed," he said.

Halleigh shook her head in disgust. "I don't understand you, Mitch," she replied with hatred laced in her voice. Any tenderness or gentleness that had once been in her voice was now null and void. She was confused, hurt, and mad. She needed to get to the bottom of this and find out what was going on. Why would Mitch be doing this to his best friend's woman?

"You were Malek's friend. He trusted you. I trusted you, Mitch. Why would you do this to us? Is this about you and me? I mean, I'm not blind. I've noticed the subtle ways you are with me. And believe me, Mitch, you are a good guy, but . . ." Halleigh's words trailed off before she continued with, "I could never be with you."

Mitch laughed charmingly, rubbing his neatly trimmed goatee as he shook his head in disagreement. He gently rubbed the back of his hand across Halleigh's cheek. "It was good, ma, but it wasn't that good." He pulled his hand away.

"I don't beef out over no broad, but let me put it to you like this, maybe if you had chosen differently, you wouldn't be in this situation. This shit don't happen to niggas like me. Only niggas like Malek. He ain't a gangster, he's a ball player. He should've stuck to the game he knew best. Believe it or not, he started this war. Now I'ma finish that nigga," Mitch said.

Mitch walked over to the door. Before exiting the room, he turned to Halleigh and said, "Now I'ma have my niggas set up the cameras in this room. The windows are armor guarded, and the door has a dead bolt. Don't be stupid, which means don't try anything stupid." Mitch turned to leave, but then had one more thing to say.

He walked back over to Halleigh. "Oh, yeah, and don't even bother wasting your time thinking about Malek. That nigga is as good as dead."

He looked down at Halleigh's stomach. "I suggest you better concentrate on keeping you and yours alive." Mitch reached to stroke Halleigh's face, but she smacked his hand away forcefully and with malice.

Mitch smiled. He couldn't help but admire her loyalty. He had known all along that her loyalty to Malek was the road block stopping him from pursuing her, which is why he never really stepped to her like he wanted to. He knew it would be in vain as long as Malek was still around. Mitch knew that Halleigh would never choose him, even after Malek's death. She loved that boy way too much, and although he didn't like it, he respected it. Any nigga in the game would have loved to have a for-real ride or die chick like Halleigh on their team.

Unfortunately, she'd never be on his, especially not now. With that final thought, Malek turned around and walked out, leaving Halleigh alone.

Although she'd managed to maintain her com-

posure while Mitch spat all that venom about Malek her way, now that he was out of sight, she began to cry her eyes out. Although he had basically promised her that she would be okay, he had also assured her that Malek was going to die. If that was the case, she didn't even care anymore whether she lived. She couldn't see herself living without Malek.

What am I going to do? she asked herself.

She could feel herself hyperventilating. With each forced breath, her heart hurt tremendously. She could feel the pit of emptiness expanding in her stomach. She wanted to scream for help, but knew better than to test Mitch. Still, she couldn't just sit there knowing that her baby's father was about to be introduced to death. She had to do something. She had to make a move. Everyone else seemed to have a plan; now it was time for her to come up with one of her own.

Chapter Two

Malek breathed heavily and his palms began to sweat profusely. He watched closely as the other people in the bank casually tended to their business all around him, not knowing what was in store for them. He began to fill out a deposit slip under a fake name as he tried to look composed. He took a deep breath and thought, *It's all or nothing.*

With that simple thought, he erased any hesitation that dwelled in his heart. He couldn't turn back. The survival of Halleigh and the child she was carrying in her womb depended on it.

Malek looked around, inconspicuously casing out the place. The bank was small, but under high surveillance. Malek had scoped out the cameras in each corner of the lobby and also the ones that were pointed directly at the tellers' drawers. He also took glance at the medium-

built, middle-aged white security guard who stood in the corner. He wasn't just a flashlight security guard either. This guy had a black .45 on his hip. Malek noticed the guard touch it every so often, patting it to make sure it was there. He was most likely a police officer moonlighting.

Malek noted the overzealous look in the security guard's eyes, as if he'd been on the job for so many years just waiting for something to jump off. He knew that the security guard wanted to be a hero. He was just waiting for the opportunity to pull that gun from the holster and shoot it, so Malek knew that if anything went wrong with his plan, the guard would be a problem.

The guard kept a watchful eye on the bank's patrons, still patting that damn gun as if it was a magnet and his hand was metal. Malek knew he was taking penitentiary chances by sticking up a bank, but the only thing on his mind was getting Halleigh's ransom. He clenched his jaws and gripped the pen tightly as he thought about Halleigh probably being tied up somewhere, hoping he would come for her, or even worse, giving up on him completely for not being there to prevent it all from happening in the first place.

Malek's eyes began to water. The guilt felt like a ton of bricks on his shoulders. He knew that it was his responsibility to protect Halleigh and his unborn child, and he had failed. What was like salt in the wound was that this wasn't even the

first time he'd failed her. What type of husband and father would he make if he couldn't keep his family safe?

The fact that Mitch had taken his most prized possession had Malek questioning his manhood. *How could I have let this happen?* he chastised himself.

Malek glanced at the door as Scratch stumbled into the bank acting drunk off his ass. In actuality, Scratch was as sober as a preacher on Easter. His demeanor was all a part of Malek's plan.

Scratch was to cause a distraction and draw the attention of the security guard while Malek robbed the place. As long as Scratch stayed in character, Malek felt like it was all a sure thing.

Scratch was staggering and talking loud. He held a brown paper bag in his hand. At first sight, it would look like was holding a 40-ounce beer bottle, but the true content of the bag was a pistol. Scratch's finger was already wrapped around the trigger. He was prepared to shoot, just in case he needed to clear a way for them to exit.

Just as planned, the guard immediately motioned toward Scratch, and that's when Malek headed to the first open teller in sight.

Malek's fitted cap was pulled low over his eyes, only showing the bottom portion of his face. He took a deep breath and walked in front of the teller, whose eyes were focused on the ruckus by the bank's entrance.

"Where in the hell is the manager?" Scratch yelled. By now everyone in the bank was looking at Scratch. "My damn ATM card just got stuck and I want my damn money!" he yelled, standing in the middle of the lobby, swaying back and forth as if he couldn't keep his balance. "I'm almost out of my drinky-drinky," he explained, "and I needs my money to gets some more."

While Scratch played his part to the nines, Malek approached the female bank teller. He was so high on his own adrenaline that he felt as if he would throw up; but he still pushed forward. Malek reached into his hoodie pocket and slowly placed the chrome .45 on the counter, his finger on the trigger.

Finally pulling her attention away from Scratch, the teller attempted to greet Malek. "How are you to—" She stopped mid-sentence after she glanced down and noticed the pistol pointed directly at her midsection.

She flinched and put her hand on her chest. "Oh my God," she whispered as her breathing became shallow.

"Just relax and keep your cool," Malek instructed in a low tone. "You know what time it is. And if you try anything funny, I'ma have to push yo shit back, okay?" Malek asked in the most subtle voice he could muster.

The teller simply nodded in fear. She was too afraid and in shock to do anything other than that as she stared down at the gun, praying and hoping that it stayed right there in its place.

"Now, I want you to give me the unmarked bills in your drawer," Malek instructed. "Put them in that big envelope right there." Malek pointed to a money deposit envelope that was among many stored behind the teller. It was the type of leather pouch that businesses used to make deposits. "Give me all hundreds and fifties, ma." Malek cocked the gun. "And if you even think about triggering the silent alarm, I'm going to make sure you're the first person I kill before the police get here."

Once again, all the teller could do was nod as her eyes watered and her breaths increased, so much so that her chest was rising up and down and Malek could clearly hear her inhaling and exhaling.

Malek noticed the pictures of the teller and her children that were placed inside her space. "Give me the money so you can go home to your kids. Now, just calm down and be smart," Malek said, trying to coach her through the robbery.

She fought back her tears while doing just as Malek had instructed.

"You're doing good." Malek briefly looked over his shoulder to make sure Scratch still had the guard's full attention.

Scratch was nearly to blows with the security guard. He was being pushed out of the bank. "Get yo mu'fuckin' hands off me, man," Scratch screamed as he tried to get back into the bank; but the burley guard wasn't having it.

The security guard was too big for Scratch to

muscle through, but he was putting up a hell of a fight and causing a scene. Even the bank manager had approached them. With all of this going on, not one person was paying attention to Malek and the teller.

After tangling with Scratch for another minute or so, the guard finally decided to just pick Scratch up and toss him out of the building like Mr. Banks used to do to Jazzy Jeff on *The Fresh Prince of Bel Air.*

Just as Scratch was hitting the ground, Malek was coming out of the building. He even smiled at the guard on his way out. The bank deposit pouch stuffed with money was under his armpit, inside his coat.

Scratch got up from the ground, fussing and cussing all the way around the corner. He was sure enough putting on a scene until he rounded the corner, flipping off the security guard as he walked out of sight.

Malek was waiting for him in the parked car. "Let's go, Scratch," he yelled out of the window as he started up the car.

Scratch hurried into the waiting vehicle. With Malek in the driver's seat, they sped off without looking back.

Before the guard even noticed that the bank had just been robbed, Malek and Scratch were gone. Malek thanked God that he had gotten out of the bank without falter. He would be no good to anyone locked up, and what he had just done was a major risk. Even so, he knew that

bank envelope didn't hold all the ransom money he needed in order to get Halleigh back.

As he drove, he got his mental together and prepared for bank job number two.

Just minutes later, Malek and Scratch were at another bank not too far from the one that they had just robbed. Working with very little time, they couldn't afford to take a break. They had to do this thing guerilla-style. Malek knew that he would have to go all out to get the half million.

Malek and Scratch were running the same game that had worked so well at the first bank, but this time they ran into a problem: a cop came in during the middle of their caper.

When he arrived at the bank, Malek had filled out a deposit slip, the same as before. He scoped the place out and noticed the security guard, this one less on guard than the one before. He was too busy checking out the female's asses to pay attention to Malek. The more Malek thought about it, he probably really didn't even need Scratch to perform his Oscar-winning role. The big-bootie women were distraction enough. Still, if it wasn't broke, there was no need to fix it, so things went on as planned.

Ironically, though, an cop came to the bank on his lunch break to cash his Friday paycheck. Just as he pulled up in front of the bank and was about to get out of his car, he heard on his police scanner about the other bank robbery that

had just taken place. He listened as the voice on the radio explained how one man caused a distraction while another man stuck up a teller.

At first he was going to drive over to the other bank location to see if they needed any assistance, but decided that since he was already at the bank, he'd go ahead and cash his check and stop by the other bank afterward. He was confident that his fellow officers had everything under control.

When the police officer got out of his car and entered the bank, he walked in and saw Scratch acting a fool. The security guard on duty was almost unable to contain the man. The officer shook his head, realizing that this security guard probably needed his help more than the officers down at the other bank.

"Where the damn manager?" Scratch yelled. "My fuckin' money didn't come out that raggedy-ass ATM machine." Scratch went on his rant as he walked over to the banker's desk in the middle of the medium-sized bank.

Malek was taking the money from the teller while the security guard was trying to calm Scratch. Just like before, all eyes were on Scratch— with the exception of the police officer, who had entered the bank in the midst of the mayhem.

At first, it was the officer's instincts to go over and try to help get the situation under control, but then he remembered the call that came over the radio describing the technique used to rob the bank earlier. He looked around, wondering

what the chances were of the same exact thing taking place just a few blocks away a few moments later. When he saw Malek and the teller—the only two people in the bank not distracted by the commotion going on between Scratch and the security guard—he knew the chances were greater than he'd initially assumed.

"Remember, just stay calm and everything will be okay," Malek reminded the nervous teller just as the police officer slipped his hand down to his gun and walked up behind Malek.

Malek tried to keep his head low. His brim covered most of his eyes. He could see the teller slipping one hand under the counter as she gave him the money with her other hand.

"What the fuck you think you doing?" Malek said in a harsh whisper. He pulled back the hammer on his gun, which lay on the counter pointed toward her.

She quickly put her hands where Malek could see them. Before he could do anything else, he heard the voice of the police officer behind him.

"Put your hands in the air where I can see them, son," the officer ordered with his gun aimed at Malek. "It's over. You're not getting out of here with this money today," the officer said sternly, but without raising his voice. The cop deliberately used a calm tone because he didn't know Malek's state of mind and didn't want his suspect to harm the innocent teller, who was already visibly frightened.

"Fuck!" Malek cursed to himself under his breath as he thought quickly about what to do. But what could he do with a gun pointed to his head? Still, that didn't keep his mind from racing for a way out—hopefully, with the money.

Within five seconds, Malek had weighed his options and decided to do what he had to do. "I'm not going to jail today," Malek whispered just before he swung around, catching the unsuspecting cop off guard with his bold actions. Malek immediately began firing his gun, hitting the cop in the midsection.

The cop managed to let off a couple of rounds, but none of them hit Malek as he ducked, dipped, and dodged toward the exit, using people as live body shields to deter the cop from firing at him for fear of shooting an innocent bystander.

The patrons in the bank went into a frenzy at the sound of the gunfire, and it became complete mayhem as screams and the sounds of a stampede caused by the panic echoed through the building. Before the security guard could react, Scratch had grabbed the guard's gun from his waist and pointed it at him. Malek saw the officer he'd shot gasping for air as he dropped his gun and held his mid-section.

"Damn, damn, damn," Malek repeated as it registered in his brain that he'd just shot a cop. He quickly exited the bank, and Scratch followed close behind.

"What the fuck happened, youngblood?" Scratch asked in confusion as he ran, almost out of breath. Scratch's eyes were bigger than golf balls. He couldn't believe what had just gone down. It was a horrible misstep that was sure to make them wanted men, especially if the cop died.

The Flint Police Department was like a gang in its own right. When one of their own went down, they held no mercy on the trespasser. Malek and Scratch would be hunted to no end, and when or if they were caught, they might not ever make it to the jailhouse. The Flint police might just deliver them to their graves.

"We weren't supposed to kill nobody. That was a fuckin' Jake!" Scratch yelled as they hopped in the car.

Malek quickly sped off. His mind was so messed up over the shooting that he didn't even stop to look to see if there were any cars coming, almost hitting a passing car as he pulled off.

"Watch it, youngblood," Scratch warned him as they weaved in and out of traffic.

"My fault," Malek said, looking through his rearview mirror to make sure they weren't being followed. He hit the steering wheel with his fist.

"He just ran up on me, man. I had to," Malek yelled as he maneuvered through traffic and made the getaway.

Scratch kept looking back to see if anyone was behind them as they sped onto the city streets,

trying to get as far away from the scene of the crime as possible. Malek periodically looked in his rearview and then focused back on the road.

"Fuck!" Malek yelled again as he repeatedly hit the steering wheel in total frustration.

Once again he peeked in his rearview and then looked at Scratch, who looked more nervous than ever. They had just stepped into the big leagues. Not only were they bank robbers, but possible cop murderers. Nothing seemed to be getting better, only worse, and they were headed down a path of destruction.